THE RECLUSIVE DRYAD

STELLA RAINBOW

Warning:

This book contains material that is intended for a mature, adult audience. It contains graphic language, explicit sexual content and adult situations.

CONTENTS

Dedicated to:
My fellow peeps in the ace community. This one's for you. <3

ONE

Alden

I loved my friends dearly, but sometimes I just wanted to lock them all in a room and throw away the key.

Luckily for me, my friends were too busy with their lives to meddle in mine, which I was just fine with.

Vo had gotten himself hired by the human chef—Trick, he'd said his name was—a few days ago, which meant he was spending practically all his time at the human's place. Memphis, Quill, and I had a bet going about whether or not Trick was Vo's mate, but I was pretty certain he was.

With Neel and Pax at the packland for school, Memphis and Orion were holed up in their bedroom for some alone time, which made it easy for me to leave the house without getting bombarded by a hundred questions about where I was going.

Ever since my friends had realized I'd been visiting Silent Creek Park with some frequency, they'd started badgering me about what I was up to, especially after I'd stopped them from tailing me there.

I'd told them I went there to shift, which was an outright lie. I hadn't shifted yet at all, though I was planning to sometime soon. I knew they had a bet going about it—they wouldn't be my best friends if they didn't—but I had no plans of revealing my agenda anytime soon.

Running my fingers through my hair and pushing them into some semblance of order, I adjusted my glasses, brushed my fingers over the horn-tip hanging from a cord around my neck—a habit I'd developed ever since I started wearing it like that—and made my way downstairs. Being as quiet as I could, I opened the door, stepped outside, and slowly closed it behind me.

It'd rained earlier today, and the air was cool, the driveway and street wet. I debated over borrowing Memphis's truck but decided against it. They'd need it to go pick up the boys later, and I didn't want to lose track of time and leave them hanging.

Instead, I walked. I loved walking, and I'd done a lot of it in my life. I'd traveled across countries on my feet—sometimes two, sometimes four—and one of the drawbacks of settling down was the lack of opportunities for going on long walks. I made it work, though.

It was how I'd ended up at Silent Creek Park the first time. It'd only been a few days since we'd moved to Mistvale, and I'd been getting restless. So, I'd gone to the park to spend some time surrounded by Mother Nature, and that was when I'd sensed them. The forest spirit—or dryad, as some called them—had claimed the park as theirs, and suddenly what I'd heard about humans not being allowed into the park had made a lot more sense. Dryads, as a rule, hated humans because they were the number one reason behind the destruction of forests and the deaths of so many forest spirits.

As a unicorn, my magic sometimes gave me insights, gut feelings about things that I'd learned not to ignore. One such insight had insisted I return to the park, and so I had. And ever since that first time, whenever I leave the park, my gut insists I return as quickly as possible.

It'd been almost two years since I'd first been to the park, and I'd been coming back to it a few times a week ever since. At first, I'd just assumed it was the pleasant atmosphere that kept pulling me, the way the air and everything in the park was tinged with a hint of magic.

I'd only recently come to the realization that it wasn't something, but *someone*. Once Memphis found his mate, I'd realized that maybe, maybe the reason I kept wanting to go back to the park was because of the person it belonged to, the forest spirit who watched over the park and guarded it.

I had yet to meet them, despite the fact that I'd been at the park every day for the past two weeks. I got the feeling they weren't a fan of people, but I wasn't going to let that stop me, not if my gut feeling was right. And I knew it was because it'd never failed me in all my centuries.

At first, I'd struggled with the idea that the forest spirit might be my mate. I'd never expected to find mine, a little because I'd already spent such a long time without them, but mostly because I'd thought something was wrong with me. I knew better now, of course. Humans and their exploration into the facets of genders and sexualities had helped me understand quite a few things about myself, but even so, I hadn't expected to find my mate so soon after Quill and Memphis—and maybe even Vo, if I was right—found theirs.

Well, technically, if the forest spirit was my mate, I'd found them before Memphis and Vo, but since I hadn't even seen my supposed-mate yet...

Blinking hard, I realized I'd walked all the way to the park completely lost in thought. Shaking my head at myself, I stepped through the threshold, unmarked by anything except the outcropping of trees and bushes. While everyone in town knew what the park was called, there were no actual markers, and I wondered if that was the dryad's doing too. Had they scared off any humans who came close enough to put up a sign?

The moment I stepped into the park, the dryad's familiar aura surrounded me. Even though I'd never seen them, I got the feeling that they could see me, that they'd been watching me. I wanted to get them to come out and talk, but so far, I hadn't been very successful.

Their presence always felt stronger when I talked to the trees and plants around me, as if they'd come closer so they could hear me better, and yet they never spoke back, or gave me even a hint of their presence, other than their aura.

I wasn't accepting defeat, though. I'd spent two years trying to earn their trust, but it was a drop in the bucket for someone as old as us, and I didn't mind spending another few years showing them they could trust me, though I hoped it wouldn't take that long.

Elian

He was here again. Just like he'd been here yesterday, and the day before that, and the day before.

He'd told me his name a long time ago, introduced himself as if he could see me, as if he wanted to know me. I'd never revealed myself to him, partly because I didn't want to, and partly because I was afraid to. I'd spent so long hiding in my trees, my bushes, and grass, that I didn't know how to stop doing it. So, I did nothing.

I stayed concealed in the trees, in the ground...everywhere. This park was my home, but it was also me. We were the one and the same, and Alden seemed to know that too because he treated every part of the park with respect and care, unlike any other supe or the few humans I allowed into my park.

"I think Vo found his mate," Alden said, settling on a fallen tree before lying down, his arms crossed under his head as he gazed up at the sky. An unfamiliar temptation to approach him, to lie over him and wrap my arms around him, coursed through me, and I pushed it back, instead focusing on the words coming out of his mouth. "He's a human, and a chef. He has a kid too, I think."

Alden talked about his family a lot. It was clear he loved them, and through him, I felt like I knew them all too. Quite a few of them visited the park too. Not as often as Alden, but enough that I remembered most of their names. If I truly met them someday, I'd know quite a lot more about them than they knew about me.

I wondered if Alden talked to them about me the way he talked to me about them. Probably not. What would he say? *I talk to this dryad every day who never says anything back?*

I could sense that we shared a connection of some kind, but I didn't know what it was. I'd spent so long as nothing but a part of my park that a lot of the emotions I should feel were...muted. Like I was underwater and my emotions were sunlight. I could see them, but I couldn't feel them, and I knew the only way to feel them properly was to take a physical form instead of just existing in the ground and trees of the park, but I hadn't been able to convince myself to do so yet, not even for the blond-haired unicorn who visited me almost daily now.

Alden chatted with 'me' for a few hours before leaving, and I spent the rest of the evening drifting through every bit of foliage in my park, making sure they were all healthy and flourishing.

The next day, when Alden returned, something was different. He'd brought something with him.

"Hey, sorry about this. I promise I won't litter. I skipped breakfast today and then realized I was hungrier than I'd thought," Alden said before taking a bite of a bread-like food with something colorful on top. It had been a long time since I'd eaten human food—I didn't need to eat. My plants kept me healthy—but something about the colorful bread Alden was eating looked mighty edible.

"I wonder if you'd like cupcakes," Alden mused as he chewed, and I wondered if that was what it was called. Then again, if I focused, I could remember some of the other supes who liked to eat at the park talking about cupcakes and pastries. I remembered thinking they looked delicious even then, though I wondered what they were made of. There were a lot of things I didn't eat, after all.

As if reading my mind, Alden continued speaking. "How about this? I'll leave one for you here before I go, and if it's still here when I come back tomorrow, I'll take the hint. Oh, and I figured you might not eat eggs and/or milk, so it's vegan, okay? You don't need to worry about that."

As I watched, Alden finished eating his cupcake before wrapping the last one in brown paper and placing it on the log of wood he'd been sitting on. "I suppose an animal could get to it too, but I think you'd stop it if you really wanted to try. I guess we'll see."

After Alden left that day, it took me a while to convince myself to leave my hideout and take a physical form. I made sure there was no one else in the park before stepping out of a tree close to the log where Alden had left the cupcake. I'd taken my human form because it was better at tasting things, and it felt strange to look at myself and see smooth brown skin and small fingers.

Reaching for the cupcake, I grabbed it quickly and stepped close to the tree, pressing my stupidly smooth back against the rough bark. My grip on the cupcake was almost too hard, and I realized I'd damaged it a little as I unwrapped it to see the smushed lump that looked a lot different than it had when Alden had wrapped it.

Carefully, I took a small bite, and my eyes widened at the explosion of sugariness on my tongue. I'd tasted the sweetest of fruits, but nothing compared to this delicacy. The cupcake was gone before I realized, and I found myself scraping the last of the creamy topping from the paper it'd been wrapped in.

Alden had given me such a delicious gift, and I realized I needed to give back. It was the right thing to do, the way things had been done in the olden days.

Carefully, I folded up the paper and placed it on the ground, laying a small rock over it so it wouldn't fly away in the breeze. Then, I sank back into the tree and traveled through the roots to the tree I was looking for. I'd hidden away all my favorite trees in a copse deep inside the park where no one else was allowed. If a human or supe came close, they saw the edge of the park instead of the copse and turned right around, but this was where I grew my food.

Stepping out of a tree in my true form, I reached up and grabbed a ripe-looking apple, carefully detaching it from the tree. Because of my magic, I could grow any plant here regardless of the season, and I made full use of that by cultivating my favorite fruits and vegetables.

I ran my palm over the apple tree in silent thanks before making my way to the log Alden preferred. There, I shifted into my human form so I could wrap the apple in the brown paper, and then I placed it on the log right where he'd left the cupcake before melting back into a tree. Now, all I had to do was wait for the new day. And Alden.

TWO

Alden

The day after leaving the cupcake for the dryad, I showed up at the park a little earlier than usual, eager to see if they'd accepted my gift.

When I saw the paper-wrapped lump sitting right where I'd left it, my shoulders slumped. With a sigh, I settled on the log and roamed my eyes over the trees in front of me.

"Guess you didn't want it, huh?" I asked as I reached for the cupcake, intending to slide it into my jacket pocket to dump later.

I frowned when the lump turned out to be harder than it should be, and my eyes widened when I unwrapped it and found something that definitely wasn't a cupcake.

The apple was bright red and shiny, nothing like the ones you found in the grocery stores. It reminded me of a long time ago, when I could pick an apple straight from a tree whenever I wanted to.

"Is this for me?" I asked like an idiot, but I didn't expect an answer, and I didn't get one.

Eyeing the apple for another moment, I took a big bite and moaned as the juicy sweetness burst across my tongue, the sharp tinge to it sending a buzz through my nerves. Fuck, I couldn't remember the last time I'd eaten an apple this good.

"Oh wow," I mumbled once I'd finished the first bite. If my friends were here, I'd have been embarrassed by the noises I'd just made, but I couldn't help myself. It just tasted so wonderful.

"I didn't see an apple tree anywhere," I mused as I admired the half-eaten apple. "But I assume there's a part of this park only you can access. A home within a home."

I took another bite of the apple as my eyes roamed around the park, admiring the way every plant looked bursting with health and joy. As a unicorn, I felt most at ease when surrounded by greenery. I was half-tempted to shift and trot around the place, but I wasn't ready for that yet.

Most people reacted a certain way when they saw my unicorn form. They wanted to reach out, touch me...check if I was real. I was the last of my kind, and some days, I really hated that.

I wouldn't mind having the dryad approach me, but I also didn't want to scare them off. From my experience so far, I got the feeling they weren't a big fan of people in general, and while they hadn't locked me out of the place yet—and I knew they could do it if they wanted to—I didn't want to risk it by trampling all over their park. At least not until we got along a little better.

I wondered what the others would think if they knew what I was up to. Memphis would probably tease me and assure me I was just talking to myself, while Quill would optimistically assure me the dryad would talk back to me any day now. Vo would want to come with me to check the dryad wasn't up to anything fishy. They were predictable, but it was one of the reasons I loved them so much.

"That apple was a hint, right? A sign that you want me around? Because that's what I'm taking it for," I said as I munched on the last of it, wishing yet again the dryad would give me some sign of their presence, of the fact that they were listening to me. I was a patient man, though, and as much as I would love to actually see them when I talked to them, I was willing to wait until they felt comfortable enough to show themself.

One benefit about talking to someone whose reaction you couldn't see was that you were able to say things you never would've otherwise. Somehow, I found myself talking about my past, something I rarely did. There was a reason unicorns were considered one of the scarcest of species, even in fairy-tales, and it wasn't a pretty reason. I was lucky to still be alive, and I tried to remember that every day.

Unlike most other supernaturals, unicorns didn't reproduce. We were asexual by nature—probably why we'd been considered 'pure' by many, though that was utter bullshit—and we could transform a deserving person into a unicorn if we wanted to. I'd never turned anyone, and I didn't plan to.

Life as a unicorn wasn't safe, and I didn't think I would've survived to see the twenty-first century if not for Vo, Quill, and Memphis. I was the last unicorn on the planet, and I intended to let the species die out with me because no one deserved to spend their life hunted, or afraid of being hunted. Been there, done that, would *not* recommend.

I'd never said these words out loud, though my friends knew most of it from the few conversations we'd had about the topic. It was easy to speak the words into the misty breeze here though, and I could almost feel the dryad around me, listening closely.

"I'm probably boring you to death with my pity party, huh?" I said at last, not expecting a reply. Instead, I lay down on the log I'd claimed as our meeting spot—so to speak—and folded my arms behind my head, staring up at the cloudy sky through the canopy of trees. It was going to rain soon. I should probably get home, even though I didn't feel like leaving.

With Vo busy with his new client—who I was certain now was also his mate—and Memphis and Orion busy with the kids, the house felt a little lonely at times. I felt less alone here, surrounded by the greenery and the dryad's faint aura. Just like the house I shared with my friends, this place felt like home.

Smiling up at the steadily darkening sky, I let my eyes fall shut, deciding a nap might be what I needed.

Elian

The smile on Alden's face when he'd seen the apple had sent sparks shooting through me and into every tree and every plant in the park. In that moment, I'd realized just how beautiful he was.

Unicorns usually were a thing of beauty, but Alden was on a whole another level. If what he'd said was true, he was the last of his kind, and while I'd never felt the need to socialize with them, I knew other dryads existed. I wondered how it was for him, knowing there was no one else like him in the world. It must feel pretty lonely. Was that why he was here, talking to me? Or could he also sense this bond we shared? A bond I still didn't understand the meaning of.

I knew that if I just shifted into my true form—or even my human form—I'd be able to understand it better, but I still wasn't ready for that yet. I'd spent centuries hiding inside—literally—my garden, and as much as I wanted to talk to Alden, it was going to take some time to gather up my courage.

I watched Alden as he slept, completely at ease. His pale curls hung around his face, draping over his folded arms. He should've removed his glasses before he fell asleep, but at least they wouldn't get damaged with him on his back.

Sensing the approaching rain, I coaxed the trees around Alden to bend forward a little more, to give him cover from the coming rain. The pitter-patter of rain started up a moment later, and a rush of joy washed through me as the flora around me cheered. They loved the rain, and so I did too.

As Alden continued napping, my trees kept him from getting wet. Soon enough, some of the little critters who made a home in the park figured out there was no rain in the little clearing Alden had claimed as his—a clearing I now didn't allow anyone else to find—and decided to wait out the rain by hunkering down there.

I had a feeling Alden's presence comforted them too. His aura was extremely pleasant, and unlike other supes and humans, he didn't feel like an outsider. He belonged in this place, belonged with me, which was as strange as it felt right. I'd never come across anyone like Alden before, and he was the first person I didn't want to let go of.

Alden slept for a few hours, and I wondered if he wasn't getting enough sleep at home. He always talked about his home and his friends fondly, so was there another reason for his sleeplessness? I wished I could ask him all the questions brewing in my mind. Soon, I promised myself.

When Alden woke up, the rain was still going strong, and he blinked a few times, dislodging his glasses as he rubbed his knuckles over his eyes. Adjusting his glasses as he sat upright, Alden turned his head up toward the sky, still blocked by the trees, before looking forward with a wide, breathtaking smile. "Thank you for keeping me from getting wet. That was very sweet of you."

Pleasure swept through me at his appreciation, and then through every tree around us. They trembled just a little from it, but their reaction wasn't noticeable with the way the wind was making them sway.

Alden stretched his arms above his head, then rested his elbows on his knees, his eyes roaming around the clearing. They lit up when he spotted the small cluster of animals at the edge, and I watched as he shifted off the log and settled on the ground, uncaring of getting his clothes dirty.

"Oh, hello there. I don't think we've met. I'm Alden," he said, holding his hand out to the squirrel who'd dared take a few steps away from the others. Alden held steady as the squirrel inched closer, and then, as if deciding he was alright, the squirrel all but leaped onto his arm, surprising a laugh out of him.

Something warm and fuzzy coursed through me as I watched Alden hold steady so the squirrel could explore him, and my urge to step out of the trees and join him grew even stronger. Just a little more time, that's all I needed. I hoped Alden wouldn't lose interest before then. I had a feeling Alden was a very patient man, but he wasn't a saint, and I shouldn't expect him to be one.

"Oh, you're a sweetheart, aren't you?" Alden murmured as he brushed his fingertip against the squirrel's head. The squirrel made a chattering sound, and then three more squirrels pulled away from the huddle and raced over to join her, climbing all over Alden's body as if he was a tree.

The wide smile on Alden's face took my breath away, and I wondered what other things I could do to make him smile.

More apples? He'd liked the one I'd left him. Maybe some other fruits? I could also convince the other animals in my park to visit Alden. He would like that, wouldn't he?

I'd never thought I could get that much joy out of making someone happy, but a laugh from Alden showed me that yes, making someone—or maybe just this particular unicorn—happy could make me feel all light and floaty. It was a feeling I wanted to experience again, because despite not being in a physical form, I felt it strongly.

When the rain finally let up, Alden decided to head home. I—and the squirrels—was sad to see him leave, but I knew he couldn't stay here. He had a home to get back to, and friends who actually participated in conversations. I couldn't expect him to stay, no matter how much I wanted it.

What I could do was make sure he had a smile on his face when he came back tomorrow. I was going to get him another gift, something that would make him happy. I'd loved the way he'd enjoyed eating that apple, the joy so clearly visible on his face, and I wanted to see it again.

Once Alden had left, I told the trees that they could rest now, and they slowly straightened up again, opening the clearing up to the skies once more. I thanked them for their help in keeping Alden warm and dry, and then traveled through the trees back to my 'home within the home' as Alden had called it. I had some gifts to gather.

THREE

Alden

The next day, I made another pit-stop at *She Bakes, He Brews* to get some treats for my dryad. For the dryad, I meant. The one who lived in Silent Creek Park. Not my dryad. Obviously.

Shaking my head at myself, I thanked Brittany, co-owner of the place, as she readied my three cupcakes. Last time, I'd brought them a strawberry cupcake because I usually bought those for myself. I liked the fruity flavors, but I figured they hadn't eaten many cupcakes, so I was bringing them a choco-late one, and a vanilla one this time.

"Want a tea to go?" Brittany asked, and I thought for a moment before nodding.

"Yes, please. A green tea with honey and lemon," I requested, and she got started on it. Before her, Hector, an alchemist who brewed tea unlike anyone else, used to handle the tea side of the shop. But after he'd found his mate—Celeste, the one and only supe therapist in our town—he'd taken a step back from the shop, leaving it to Iris—the baker—and her girlfriend and mate, Brittany. I missed Hector's tea, but Brittany had learned the brews from him, so while it didn't have his magic, it wasn't bad either.

"There you go," Brittany said as she slid my order across the counter, and I thanked her as I handed over my credit card. Once the payment was done, I took my paper bag of goodies, and my tea before strolling out of the mall the locals called TOSS—The One Stop Shops.

As I walked to the park, my thoughts returned to yesterday, when I'd woken up to the sound of heavy rain. I'd been surprised to find myself completely dry, but then I'd looked up and realized the trees around me had all bowed forward, shielding me with their leaves and branches until not a single drop of rain could reach me. I had no doubts the dryad had convinced them to do that, and I'd felt so fucking pleased. The apple could've simply been a gesture of reciprocation, but keeping me dry? That had felt like care. The dryad cared about me, even if they weren't ready to show themself.

Like always, I felt completely at ease the moment I stepped into the park, and a smile graced my lips at that. I kept up my steady pace as I headed toward my spot, though a part of me wanted to race forward.

When I stepped into the clearing, the bushes practically parting themselves for me, I jerked to a halt as my eyes fell on the log. I almost dropped the bag of cupcakes in surprise, but then I recovered and resumed walking.

Sitting down in my usual spot, I balanced the paper bag and takeaway cup of tea beside me, my eyes still stuck on my new gifts. There was another apple, two strawberries, and four perfectly round, perfectly shiny blueberries. My mouth watered at the sight of them, and I'd picked one up and stuck it into my mouth before I knew.

"Oh, holy fuck," I groaned as the sweet, slightly tart juice filled my mouth, overwhelming all my senses with its sheer perfection. I could write poems about how magnificent it tasted. If I had any talent at all, that was.

Once I'd licked up all the dripping blueberry juice off my fingers, I wiped my hand on my jeans before taking a sip of my tea.

"I brought you two cupcakes this time. The brown one is chocolate, and the white one is vanilla. Maybe you could figure out a way to let me know which one you liked better?" I asked the trees around me before taking another sip of tea. The weather was much warmer today, and birds chirped in the trees. I wondered where the squirrels from yesterday were, and if they planned to visit me again.

Once I'd finished my tea, I placed the empty Styrofoam cup at the end of the log to take with me later and grabbed the apple, blinking when I realized it felt rough against my palm.

Turning it around, I stared at the apple for a moment before realizing there were letters carved into it. Upside-down letters. I turned the apple and read the wobbly writing. E-L-I-A-N.

"Elian," I murmured before looking up at the trees. "Is that your name, Elian?" I asked, and though there was no reaction of any kind, I still felt like they'd heard me and agreed. "It's a beautiful name," I murmured, rubbing my thumb over the engraved letters.

"I almost don't want to eat this apple now, but I wouldn't want you to think I don't appreciate your gift," I said softly before biting into the juicy fruit. I probably could've saved it for later, but I didn't want it to go bad.

Once I'd finished eating, I lay back on the log in a familiar routine. Unlike the other days, though, I could feel the dryad's—Elian, I reminded myself—presence closer than usual. Were they getting used to having me around?

"Whenever you're ready, I'd love to share a meal with you. I'd eat the fruits you bring me, and I'd bring you whatever cupcakes you like the best. We could have a picnic. Wouldn't that be fun?"

Something shifting in the bushes made me snap my head up hopefully, but instead of Elian, one of the squirrels skittered into the clearing, her hands clasped in front of her as she eyed me for a moment.

Apparently deeming me safe, she raced over and climbed up the log and onto my stomach before I could get a word out of my mouth.

"Hello, there," I said once she was seated on my chest, and she chittered at me before racing off me and to my small collection of fruits. She reached for a blueberry before turning her eyes to me. When I didn't react, she grabbed it, holding it between her tiny hands.

I waited for her to race off into the trees or gobble it up—did squirrels even eat fruits like that?—but instead, she climbed back onto my chest, holding the blueberry out to me.

"Oh. Is it for me?" I asked, dumbfounded, and the squirrel stayed where she was.

"Thank you," I said, taking the fruit from her. If I didn't know better, I'd think she was Neya, Raphael's familiar. She was much smarter than an average squirrel; that was for sure.

Or maybe Elian could talk to her somehow? Maybe they could ask her to do things. While I knew a lot about dryads, I didn't know everything. I didn't know the true extent of their powers, and I imagined it was greater than I'd assumed.

Elian

Alden knew my name. He knew my name, and he'd said it out loud.

It'd been a long time since I'd heard my name said out loud, and it felt wonderful, especially because it was Alden uttering it.

I'd snuck close to him, closer than I'd ever been, so I could see his reaction to the apple properly. I'd loved the way he'd said my name, and I'd wanted to show myself at that moment more than anything I'd ever wanted.

Unfortunately for me, I couldn't always do the things my heart wanted. My mind wouldn't allow it, filling me with unnecessary and unsubstantiated fears that held me back.

I wished I wasn't like that. I wished I could just step out of this tree and approach Alden, talk to him the way he talked to me. But no matter how hard I tried, I just couldn't do it.

"I had an idea the other night, a way where we could hang out with maybe a little less pressure for you," Alden said, pulling me out of my thoughts.

He was still on his back, his eyes on the sky as he spoke, as if he could somehow sense my tumultuous thoughts and didn't want to scare me.

"I don't know if it'll work, but I'll try it soon. We'll see," he said, and then his eyes slowly drifted shut.

Like yesterday, he fell into a peaceful nap, and I convinced a few of the trees around him to give him shade from the sun. He had such pale skin, and while I knew the sun couldn't harm him the way it would a human, I'd still feel better if it wasn't shining straight onto his face.

Letting myself sink into the park, I filled myself with what my trees and plants were feeling, looking for anything that might need my help.

A few weeds needed to be convinced to let the flowers around them grow, and another dying plant had to be coaxed into getting better. I let the humdrum of my daily routine carry me off, and by the time I returned to Alden's clearing, he was gone, the paper bag of cupcakes sitting on his log.

Shifting into my human form, I made sure the area around me was inaccessible to anyone before approaching the log. Taking a seat, I placed my palm on the dead wood. I could almost feel Alden's presence on it, his warmth, his light.

With a sigh, I opened the bag and pulled out a brown cupcake, eyeing the brown cream doubtfully before taking a small bite.

My eyes widened at the burst of sweet, creamy deliciousness, and I chewed quickly before taking another big bite. I'd finished the cupcake in three bites, and I found myself licking my fingers much like Alden had licked his earlier.

Digging into the bag, I pulled out the other cupcake. This one was brown on the bottom with white on top. Vanilla, he'd called it. Eyeing it thoughtfully, I took a small bite. It wasn't as...vibrant as the other one, or fruity like the one before, but I liked it even better than the others. It was softer, more sublime in its sweetness. I liked it a lot.

Thinking over how to tell this to Alden, I pursed my lips as I stared at the empty paper bag.

An idea struck, and I flattened the bag onto the log before picking up a few pebbles from the ground. Then, I spelled out a big V on top of the bag, pinning it to the log with the pebbles at the same time.

Early tomorrow morning, I'd get some fruits for Alden, maybe some grapes. I contemplated growing a few exotic fruit trees so I could offer him a variety, and then shook the idea off. I needed to get a grip on myself.

Maybe it was because it'd been such a long time since I'd interacted with another supernatural. I'd forgotten how to socialize without overdoing it. It wasn't because Alden was special. Not at all.

Alden wasn't the only supe who visited my park, but he was the only one who'd ever talked to me. The others, they always came with someone else—usually their mates—and they only talked to each other, though I was sure they sensed my presence. I never tried to hide it, though I did make sure they couldn't sense exactly where I was.

The difference between Alden and other supes was simple. I didn't want to talk to the other supes. I didn't want them to spend every day in my park. I would never offer them fruits from my personal garden.

Similarly, the other supes would never strike up a conversation with me. They would never bring me cupcakes, or wish to spend some time in the park all on their own.

No one was quite like Alden, and that was probably why I didn't like anyone else. Alden was special, and I needed to get myself together so I could finally approach him. I was tired of hanging back, of hiding in the shadows.

FOUR

Alden

It'd been a few weeks since we started swapping gifts. So far, Elian had brought me apples, blueberries, grapes, blackberries, and a few other fruits. I never knew what to expect when I walked into the park, but I always knew there would be something waiting for me.

After trying out more than a dozen flavors, Elian had decided vanilla was still his favorite. I'd gotten used to our way of communication, and Elian had used the pebbles to tell me a few more things. Like the fact that he used he/him pronouns.

I realized that we'd gotten stuck in a pattern, though, and I had a feeling I was the one who needed to push forward. I'd had an idea about my next step weeks ago, but I'd been putting it off because I was afraid of scaring Elian. I couldn't wait any longer, not if I wanted to actually see Elian one day.

"Hey, Elian," I greeted as I stepped into the familiar clearing, smiling at the small collection of fruits waiting for me. Placing the cupcakes on the log, I took a seat, and a small "Oh!" of surprise slipped past my lips when I realized there was something more waiting for me.

I picked up the small bunch of flowers, their fragrance mellow and sweet. The small stalks were tied together with vines and fashioned into a bouquet, and I loved it. I couldn't remember the last time someone had given me flowers, and it meant quite a lot to me. Running my fingers over the petals, I realized I wasn't the only one ready for the next step.

"Thank you so much for these, Elian," I said, glancing at the trees. Carefully placing the flowers on the log, I started on the fruits, wishing Elian was physically here so that we could eat together. Someday soon, hopefully.

Once I'd finished, I stood up and scanned the trees, sensing Elian draw closer even if I couldn't see him. I knew he was everywhere in this park. It was his domain, and he could be inside any tree or flower, as long as it was connected to the earth.

"Remember that idea I had? Well, I think I'm finally ready to give it a try," I said, straightening my shirt nervously. I'd shifted into my true form hundreds of times before, but somehow this felt like the most important time of my life.

Taking a deep breath, I slowly relaxed my magic, allowing myself to sink into my four-legged form. It felt like getting out of a particularly constricting pair of jeans, and I shook myself, swishing my tail as I got my bearings.

In this form, I could *feel* the park around me much more deeply. I could sense individual plants, and the bits of magic coursing through them. I could also sense exactly which tree Elian was inside of. I took a couple steps toward it before stopping, not wanting to scare him off.

I tried to broadcast comfort and assurance, keeping my head lowered as I waited hopefully.

For a few minutes, there was nothing but the sound of birds chirping and the odd animal rushing around the park. But then, I heard it. Movement, shifting of bushes in front of me. I resisted the urge to look up, holding myself steady as my tail swished in anticipation.

Even though I wouldn't allow myself to see him, I could feel Elian drawing closer. His aura was so much thicker now that he was in a physical form, and it was so tempting to just look up. But I didn't. I held still and didn't breathe as I waited for him to come closer.

The piercing sound of a baby crying filled the air, and Elian's presence disappeared with a snap. I jerked upright, scanning the trees around me, but he was gone.

Digging my hoofs into the ground with a huff, I turned around and stalked toward the sound. There weren't many supes in Mistvale with a baby, but I had a feeling I knew exactly who I would encounter.

As I stepped through the trees, the familiar aura of family greeted me as Vo and his mate Trick came into focus, with Vo busy consoling Trick's daughter, Lena.

Trick looked up when I came into view, and his eyes went wide as he gawked at me. Oh hell. While even the supe members of our clan sometimes got caught up in the fact that I was a unicorn, it was a whole different ball game with humans.

Unicorns were one of the most popular supes in the human world, even if they were mostly adored by kids and very different from what unicorns actually were like.

I shifted into my human form as Trick continued staring, and adjusted my glasses.

"Vo, I didn't know you were coming to the park today," I said pointedly. Memphis and Vo had been trying to figure out what I was doing for weeks. I'd already caught Memphis following me a few times, and I suspected Vo had been hoping to 'catch me in the act,' so to speak.

"Yeah, it was a last-minute thing. We were all getting a little stir-crazy. Alden, this is Trick and Lena. Trick, this is Alden."

I held my hand out, and Trick took it, shaking it quickly. "It's a pleasure to meet you, Alden. Vo has told me a lot about you."

"Likewise," I said with a smile before glancing over at the little girl in Vo's arms. "Hello, Lena."

Lena gave a happy shriek, and I smiled at her before sneaking a glance at our surrounding. I couldn't sense Elian, but I suspected he was close by, observing us from one of the nearby trees.

Vo and Trick managed to drag me into a conversation, and since I had no good excuse—the last thing I wanted was to prove Vo right by telling him I was meeting someone at the park—I had to join their picnic and spend a few hours with them.

They finally left a little before sunset, and I breathed a sigh of relief before racing back to my clearing.

The cookies I'd brought for Elian today were gone, but unlike every other time, there were no fruits waiting for me.

Elian

I'd been so distracted by the magnificent aura Alden exuded in his true form that I hadn't even noticed the newcomers.

After weeks of struggle, I'd gathered up the courage to show myself to Alden, only to be foiled by a couple of supes and a human.

I'd watched them from a distance without listening to their conversation. But even so, it hadn't taken me long to figure out who they were.

Alden had told me all about his gargoyle friend and the human he was protecting—the human who was his mate. The bond they shared was the only reason the human had even been able to come inside my park, but if I hadn't been so distracted by Alden, I would've known the moment he first stepped in.

Once it was clear Alden would be spending some time with his friend, I retreated back to our clearing just in time to stop the squirrels from taking off with the cookies Alden had brought for me today.

In my human form, I sat on the log and munched through them while I waited for Alden to finish up. Maybe he wouldn't even come back. He must've been tired of keeping up a one-sided conversation for so long, right? As much as he assured me he could be patient, was it fair to him to make him wait?

When I'd finished the cookies and Alden and his friends were still exactly where I'd last seen them—having a picnic, of all things—I decided I'd gather some fruits for Alden instead of just sitting around and waiting for him. Maybe I could get some extra apples for his friends. I'd keep the berries for him, though. He loved those.

Sinking back into the ground, I made my way back to my garden and started plucking some ripe apples. I'd only broken off three of them when I sensed the others leave. I could feel Alden making his way back to his clearing, so I picked up the apples and made my way back to him.

"I'm sorry," Alden's voice reached me through the clearing, and I paused. Sorry? What was he apologizing for?

"I didn't know they were going to be here, and I didn't know if you wanted me to tell them about u—about you," Alden said, stumbling over his words, and I shifted closer.

Carefully, I rolled one of the apples into the clearing, making sure to keep myself out of view. The earlier interruption had sapped some of my courage, and I didn't think I could give it another shot. I'd loved seeing him in his unicorn form, though. I wanted to do that again.

Taking the second apple, I scratched a few words into the shiny surface before rolling it toward Alden as well.

Try again tomorrow?

"Oh! Yeah, yeah, we can do that," he said after a moment, and I relaxed slightly, sinking into a nearby tree.

"Sorry. I just came back, and the cookies were gone, but there were no fruits, so I thought I'd done something wrong," Alden said, ducking his head down as if embarrassed. I wanted to assure him it was okay. Instead, I just watched as he gathered himself and settled onto the log to snack on his apples. How he could eat them both after having a picnic lunch with his friends, I didn't know. But I was glad to see him eating.

I always enjoyed watching him consume fruits from my garden. It made me feel like I'd done some good, like I'd provided for him.

"I better get going," Alden said with a glance at the sky once he'd finished. "The kids will head to bed soon, and I don't want to miss out on some uncle time." He smiled as he said the words, and I could see just how much he adored those kids.

He'd told me all about them, of course. Neel and Pax. They were his friends' sons, and he lived with all of them. I tried not to think about what that meant for me, for *us*, if the bond we shared was in fact a mate bond. I'd been so close to finding out today. Just a few more steps and we'd have been face-to-face for the first time ever.

Tomorrow, I promised myself. Tomorrow, I'd be brave. I wanted to be brave. I wanted to touch Alden, to run my fingers through his beautiful, rainbow-colored mane. I wanted to brush my palm down his flank, to rest my forehead against his and share the same air with him. And I was going to do it all. Tomorrow.

Alden walked over to the edge of the clearing, reached out a palm, and rested it on the bark of the tree I hid inside. So close. He was so close.

"See you tomorrow, Elian," he whispered softly before turning around and walking away.

I watched him leave, flitting from tree to tree to follow his exit. When he was finally past the boundary and I couldn't sense him anymore, I turned around and went back to my garden. Tending to my trees, and then the whole park, I let my thoughts drift, let *myself* drift, until I was nothing more than just another part of this beautiful place.

Night came, and the sound of crickets replaced the bird chirps as they woke up and started moving about.

Three owls—frequent nightly visitors of mine—flew around the park, hunting and playing around. Two of them were shifters, and the third was a familiar. A strange trio, but guessing from the age of the shifters, I suspected the familiar belonged to one of their parents.

Like every visit, I watched over them while they were here, and once they were gone, I finally let myself drift off into sleep.

FIVE

Alden

The next day, I was up way before sunrise. I'd barely slept, too excited about today to let my brain rest. Once it was an acceptable time to get up, I jumped into the shower.

I was dressed and ready to tackle the day in record time, and I'd almost managed to sneak out of the house when Memphis and Orion came down the stairs.

"Heading out early?" Memphis asked just as I'd unlocked the door, and I turned to look at him. Orion gave a shake of his head, mumbled something about coffee, and headed off toward the kitchen without paying either of us any mind.

"Yeah," I answered Memphis as I turned to face him, and he smiled.

"Vo was right, wasn't he? You're seeing someone. At the park," he said, and I sighed. I still didn't know if Elian was okay with me telling the others about him. I didn't like keeping secrets from my friends, my *family*. But I also didn't want to lose Elian's trust when I'd just started gaining it. Then there was the fact that I wasn't even a hundred percent sure he was my mate.

"No," I answered slowly, and Memphis rolled his eyes.

"You're a shit liar, Alden. Don't worry. I'm not going to try to follow you again," he said with a chuckle, and I smiled despite myself.

"You better not," I said with a raised brow, and he held his palms up in surrender.

"I'll stay out of your way, I promise. If you need any help with...anything at all, let me know. Okay?"

"Of course," I assured him with a smile, then thought better of it and gave him a quick hug. "Thank you."

Memphis hugged me back, then kissed my forehead. "Yeah, yeah. Now go so I can enjoy my morning coffee in peace."

"Yes, sir," I said as I pulled back, and he gave me a wave as I unlocked the door and stepped outside. It looked like it would rain again today, but I was sure Elian wouldn't let it touch me, just like last time.

As had become my routine these days, I walked to TOSS first and got a small selection of cupcakes for Elian and me, along with tea for myself. I needed to figure out if Elian liked tea. Maybe I could get one for him to try too?

We were already going to try something new today, so maybe another time. I had a feeling Elian could get easily over-whelmed, and I wanted to avoid that if I could.

Taking my purchases, I walked to the park, sipping my tea as the sun slowly brightened up the town. Dew glistened on the leaves, and bird chirps filled the air as everyone and everything greeted the new day. A slight breeze washed across the street, and I closed my eyes for a moment to breathe everything in. God, I loved Mistvale.

I'd spent a long time roaming all over this planet, both be-fore and after I met Memphis and the others. But no other place had ever felt as good, as *right* as Mistvale. This was my home, my forever home.

Or maybe this is, I thought as I stepped through the park's threshold and the familiar sense of comfort surrounded me. I made my way through the trees almost on autopilot, my focus on the way the bark of the trees felt under my fingers—rough, wet, familiar.

When I reached the clearing, I found a few apples waiting for me. Placing the paper bag of cupcakes on the log—I'd thrown the tea cup in the trash already—I stood upright and took a few steps toward the trees. I was too eager to eat anything right then. I guess my patience did have limits after all.

"Hey, Elian. Yesterday, you said we can try again today. I'd like to do that. You don't have to hurry, okay? Just take your time and approach me when you feel comfortable," I said, my words rushing together.

Pulling my phone out of my pocket, I placed it on the log beside the cupcakes. Trick's stalker was still out there, and I wanted to be on alert in case Vo needed my help.

Turning back to the trees, I took a deep breath and relaxed my magic, shifting into my true form. I shook my head to get my mane out of my eyes, and scanned the trees around me.

Hearing some bushes shift, I placed one hoof in front of the other and bowed forward, waiting for Elian to come closer. I kept my breaths steady, and my ears twitched at the smallest of sounds from our surroundings.

Elian's aura was so much clearer to me in this form, and I could sense his curiosity, hesitation, and excitement. I waited with bated breath as the trees in front of me rustled, as I heard and felt Elian come closer. So close, he was so close.

Dark brown roots appeared in my view, and when Elian took another step, I realized it was him. Elian, in his true form. I was tempted to look up, needing to see the rest of him, but I held myself steady. And waited.

After what felt like an eternity had passed, Elian raised his hand, filling my vision with the vines that hung from the length of his arm, and placed it on my head, right above the spot where my horn met my forehead.

In a moment, the last of my doubts disappeared as recognition flared through me.

Mate, my gut screamed at me, and I almost fell over in relief. All this time, I'd been right. This beautiful, wonderful dryad was my mate.

Elian rubbed his palm on my head, and I loved it, despite the scratchy, rough feel. Slowly, I raised my head so I could see him, all of him, and my breath caught in my lungs when I finally got my first good look.

I'd seen dryads before, of course. But every dryad looked different. They were connected to their lands, and their appearance reflected that.

Elian's skin was made up of dark brown bark, his hands and the backs of his arms covered with a thin layer of soft-looking green moss. Green vines hung from the length of his arms, and roots sprouted out of his legs from his knees and everything below.

But his best feature was his face. A few shades lighter than the rest of him, his face resembled the way a tree looked beneath a layer or two of bark. Smooth and soft brown, it looked utterly touchable. Pale green eyes peered out, showing off the nervousness Elian seemed to be trying to hide.

I pressed my head harder into his palm in an attempt to comfort him, and his eyes softened as a slight smile appeared on his face. My eyes flicked to the top of his head, where instead of hair, more vines shot out of his scalp, along with tiny little flowers that dotted them, making him look like something out of a fairy tale.

"Hello, Alden," Elian said, the first words he'd ever said to me. His voice was rough, scratchy, and the best thing I'd ever heard. This time, it would be Elian talking and me listening. Perfect.

Elian

Alden was a magnificent creature.

I'd never seen a coat as pure white as his, and his colorful mane stood out against the white canvas. His eyes were a darker shade of lavender than in his human form, the color more pronounced, more ethereal.

I ran my palm down the slope of his face, and he closed his eyes, pushing into my touch.

"You're beautiful," I whispered, and Alden opened his eyes to meet mine. It felt surreal to be on the other side of our interactions, to be the one who did the speaking. But at the same time, the fact that Alden couldn't talk back somehow made it easier to talk to him.

I took a step back so I could get a good look at all of him, and the leather cord hanging around his neck caught my eye. I'd seen it around his neck in his human form, but I'd assumed it was just a piece of jewelry. Now, I could see that the pointy pendant attached to the cord was in fact the tip of his horn.

If I remembered correctly, a unicorn's horn was where their magic was most concentrated. Who had dared to break Alden's? And why? How could anyone ever think to hurt a unicorn?

Walking around Alden, I picked up one of the apples I'd brought for him and held it out to him. He made a soft, happy sound as he stepped closer and chomped down the apple in one big bite.

Laughing softly, I scratched behind his ear, and he bowed forward, bumping the edge of his horn against my shoulder.

"Thank you," I said after I'd been petting him for a minute, and he raised his head before tilting it to the side, the question clear in his eyes. "People rarely talk to me when they visit the park, even the supes who can sense me. Well, honestly, I prefer it that way. Or I used to think I did. But I've enjoyed our conversations, and I'm really grateful for your patience."

Alden gave a soft whinny before licking my palm with his long, broad tongue, and I laughed as I patted his side. "I really like you, Alden. I didn't realize what our bond was before, but now I know for sure. I didn't think I'd ever discover my mate, you know? Most dryads don't because we're tethered to our land, and unless our mate walks right through our territory, we'd never find them. I'm lucky you came to the park, though I suppose your magic led you here."

Alden gave a very human-like nod, and I chuckled. This was the first time I was talking in ages, and yet it didn't feel as awkward as I'd thought it would. I was sure it had a lot to do with the person. I already felt comfortable around Alden, though I knew I still had a ways to go. I wanted to be able to talk to him when we were both in forms that allowed for speaking, where there weren't any more walls between us.

Slowly, I stepped to Alden's side and wrapped my arms around his neck, resting my forehead on his muscular shoulder covered in a feather-soft coat. Alden gave a deep rumble that I could feel vibrating from his body to mine, and I soaked the sound in as I closed my eyes, breathing in the sweet, clean scent of his coat. Alden smelled like spring and happiness, like he belonged right here in my park, with me.

We spent the whole day with our roles reversed, and Alden listened attentively as I told him about myself, about my park.

Recalling our earlier conversations, I mentioned some of the people he'd talked about. Even though I never interacted with any of them, I knew about quite a few of the members of the Mistvale clan. My park was visited by most, if not all of them, and I'd learned quite a few things merely by being around them.

I kept most of the things to myself, but I happily shared a few unharmful tidbits with Alden—like the slang a young dragon named Cam had introduced me to, or the two cat shifters who loved chasing each other through my park—and he seemed to find immense pleasure from the anecdotes.

I realized when I retreated to the trees and Alden shifted back to his human form that evening that most of what I'd said had been about others. While Alden talked about his friends, he'd also told me about himself, and I didn't think I'd reciprocated very well.

It wasn't that I didn't want to tell Alden about myself. It was just that the life I'd led was very...boring. I'd been tethered to this park from the moment I came into being, while Alden had spent his years roaming all over the world. As similar as we were, we had just as many differences, and I was afraid that he wouldn't be as fascinated with me once he realized just how small my world was. Maybe he already knew and didn't care, or maybe he didn't. Either way, I didn't want to prove him right.

I'd already eaten the snacks Alden had brought me, so when Alden had left, I retreated to my garden and whiled away the next few hours tending to my plants, talking to them and making sure they were all growing well. It was soothing work, and as I worked, some of the anxiety I'd been feeling slowly drifted away.

SIX

Elian

If I had to describe the past few weeks in one word, I'd say they were...educating. Alden and I had spent every day together, sometimes with him in his human form and me in the trees, and others with him in his unicorn form and me doing the talking. I'd managed to share a little more about myself, and if anything, Alden appeared more interested than ever.

Which was why I was now filling all my trees with second-hand worry. For the first time in weeks, Alden hadn't shown up. It'd been a while since the time he usually came at, and I had no idea where he was. Had something happened?

Was he in danger? Or was it his friends? Had the stalker who'd been troubling Vo and his mate done something to them?

Every new question brought a healthy dose of worry with it, and there was nothing I could do to alleviate it. I didn't have one of those modern contraptions Alden used—I'd refused his repeated offers to get me one, which I now regretted—and I didn't think I could make myself leave.

While I *was* tethered to my park, I could leave it. I couldn't go too far, but maybe it was worth a try? I didn't even know where Alden lived, so I wasn't sure what I would achieve, but I didn't know how long I could just sit here and wait.

In the end, I decided to wait a day before doing anything drastic. I didn't know if I was trying to be sensible or if I was just a coward, but I didn't feel guilty enough to change my mind either way.

A while after night had fallen, I sensed something. Him. Alden.

The relief I felt had me racing across the park, skipping from tree to tree and then materializing into my true form moments before I came face-to-face to him a few steps from the entrance.

Alden jumped in surprise, and then a wide smile spread across his face when he realized it was me. "Elian!"

I threw my arms around him and pulled him into a hug, breathing him in for a moment before my brain caught up with the rest of me and I dropped my hold around him, taking a cautious step back.

Alden's hand wrapped around my arm before I could melt into the trees, his eyes dark and gleaming in the dark. "Elian, wait. Stay. Please?"

I stared at him, examining his face as I tried to read him. Alden had always been in his unicorn form when I showed myself earlier, which meant I couldn't read his reaction to me. It was why I preferred it that way. But now, here we were, but all I could see on Alden's face was recognition...and happiness. He didn't care what I looked like, just that I was here.

"Okay," I said in a low voice, trying to keep its scratchy quality subdued.

Still keeping a hold on my hand, Alden led the way to our clearing, and every plant and tree in our path cheered right up once they realized Alden was back and I'd stopped fretting.

"I'm sorry if I worried you," Alden said as we stepped into the clearing, and I followed suit when he sat down on the log, turning a little so I could face him.

While it was still dark, the sky wasn't cloudy tonight, and here in the clearing, the moon shone directly on us, making Alden's porcelain skin almost sparkle. If a human saw him at this moment, even they would have to admit there was something magical about Alden, something ethereal.

Compared to him, I was nothing more than a talking tree, and while I noticed our differences every single minute, they'd never been as obvious as right then. And yet, for some reason I just couldn't understand, Fate had decided we belonged together. I wasn't stupid enough to doubt Fate, but I wished I could understand her reasons better. Maybe then I wouldn't feel so lacking.

"Are you okay?" I asked, to get out of my head and also because his absence had really concerned me. It'd also made it clear I needed to make some changes if I didn't want to lose Alden, and I needed to make them yesterday.

"I'm fine, Elian. I'm sorry I worried you, truly. My friends decided we needed to visit Vo and Trick, cheer them up, and I couldn't pull away long enough to come let you know," Alden said, sliding his palm from my arm to my hand. He linked our fingers together, his smooth, warm skin against my rough one.

"It's not your fault. Maybe I should have a phone. It would make it easier to stay in touch and communicate," I said, and Alden smiled.

"Really? You mean that?" he asked, and I nodded. While I hated anything human-made, I cared about Alden more, and if doing this would keep us both from worrying about the other, then I couldn't say no.

"Yes. I don't want to worry like that, ever. I don't even know where your house is, Alden. Even if I'd managed to leave the park, I wouldn't have been able to find you. Having a phone would've helped me avoid all of that," I said, and Alden sighed.

"I'm truly sorry. I never wanted to scare you like that," he said, his eyes latching onto our joined hands. He linked his fingers with mine, and I worried he'd hurt himself from my rough skin, but he was tougher than he looked. The warmth of his skin seeped into mine, and for a few minutes, we were both completely fascinated by the play of our fingers against each other.

"Are Vo and Trick okay?" I asked after a few minutes of silence, and Alden looked up with a smile.

"Yeah, they're doing great. Vo's finally learning to cook, which surprised the shit out of us, but it makes him happy, so we're glad," Alden said, and then proceeded to tell me about the stew Vo had made and how delicious it was.

Before, I'd had practically no interest in human food, but now Alden had me hooked to cupcakes and pastries, so much so that I wondered what other foods I might enjoy. Alden would help me find out, I realized with a shot of happiness as I gazed at his smiling face, and I couldn't wait.

Alden

I stumbled into the house at six in the morning, after promising Elian I'd be back after a change of clothes with some new treats for him to try. He'd decided sometime during our all-night-long conversation that he wanted to try out other human foods. His only condition was that the food be vegan, which I understood.

I yawned as I blindly headed toward the stairs. While I didn't need as much sleep as a human would, I did need some, and I hadn't slept since I woke up yesterday morning. Maybe I'd grab a nap at the park later.

Elian's worry for my well-being had surprised me a little. While we both knew about the bond we shared, neither of us had mentioned it since Elian acknowledged it the first day I'd shifted into my unicorn form in front of him.

While we spent our days together, we did nothing more than talk and be in each other's company. For me, that was enough, but I couldn't help but wonder if it was enough for Elian.

I knew a few asexual people, and one of them was mated to one of my best friends. Of all of the ace people I knew, none of them were mated to another ace person. Their mates were allosexual, and while I would never pry into their personal business—not that Quill had any problem sharing details with us even when we didn't want to hear them—I was a little curious about how they made it work.

Approaching the topic with Elian was a bridge I wasn't ready to cross yet, though I knew there was only so long we could spend like this before one of us broke.

"There you are!"

I jumped and almost tripped down the three stairs I'd managed to climb in my half-sleepy, half-introspective daze, and I clung to the banister as I glared at Memphis. He stood at the top of the stairs, perfectly put together with his usual aura of confidence and sensuality clinging to him like an armor.

"Where have you been?" Memphis demanded as he descended the stairs, his eyes scanning me from head to toe. "If I didn't know better, I would say this was a walk of shame," he commented with a raised brow as he reached the step above mine. He tugged at my wrinkled shirt, emphasizing that he knew I was in the same clothes as the night before.

Then his brow shot up even higher as he reached for my face. I stared at him as his fingers brushed my hair, and then he was holding a dry leaf in front of my face.

"You were at the park," he declared without a shred of doubt in his voice, and I nodded because I knew better than to lie to him.

Pursing his lips, he grabbed my arm and led me back downstairs and into the kitchen. Pushing me toward a barstool, he walked around the counter and started fussing with the coffee machine before opening a cabinet and pulling out my favorite tea. He turned the kettle on before rounding on me, and crossed his arms over his chest.

"Vo was right, wasn't he?" Memphis asked, still in that tone that said he already knew the answer but wanted me to admit it. "You found them. Your mate."

I chewed on my lower lip as I stared at him, and wondered if Elian would mind if I said anything. Honestly, I was tired of keeping it a secret from my best friends. At first, I hadn't told them because I hadn't been sure what connection Elian and I shared was, but now that I knew, I wanted to talk about it with someone.

"Yeah," I said finally, and Memphis nodded as the kettle gave a beep.

Pulling my mug from its shelf, Memphis filled it, dropped a tea bag in, and slid the mug to me before grabbing his own mug and walking over to the coffee machine.

Once he had his drink, he joined me on the other side, hopping onto the stool beside mine and turning so he was facing me before swiveling my stool with his feet.

"Please don't tell the others just yet," I said before he could ask anyone, and he tilted his head, his black curls tumbling across his forehead.

"Why not?" he asked, and I was glad to detect only curiosity in his tone.

"Well, he's not much of a people person, and if the others knew..." I trailed off, and Memphis smirked.

"If they caught wind of it, everyone would be at the park tomorrow," he said when I couldn't find the right words, and I laughed.

"Yeah. Exactly."

"It's the forest spirit, isn't it? He's your mate," Memphis said, and I stared at him. How did he know everything?

"Don't worry, Alden. I didn't follow you if that's what you're thinking. I just put together the clues: you only ever meet at the park, he's not fond of people, and I feel like I know all the other supes in Mistvale at least by sight. The only one I've never seen—as far as I know—is the forest spirit."

"His name is Elian," I admitted, and Memphis smiled.

"It's a great name. I look forward to meeting him whenever he's ready," he said, and I was tempted to jump off my stool and hug him.

Why the hell not? I thought as I slid off my seat and wrapped my arms around him with him still sitting on the stool. It was the only reason he was taller than me, and he made full use of his temporary height advantage to rest his chin on my head and tuck me in as he returned the hug. My friends were my family, and I was glad I'd finally told Memphis about Elian. I would share with the others soon, but Vo needed to focus on Trick and Lena right now, and telling Quill—and therefore his mates Joy and Tate—would mean telling the whole clan, so for now, Memphis had to be enough.

After a minute, I pulled away and we returned to our drinks, both of us content to talk about other things, simpler things.

SEVEN

Alden

After grabbing a shower and a change of clothes, I made myself another cup of tea and sipped on it while I cooked pancakes for the others. They hadn't come down yet, and I was hoping to take off before they did.

While I'd managed to tackle Memphis's questions, I didn't want to be interrogated by anyone else today if I could avoid it.

One the pancakes were ready, I packed a few and filled a tumbler with hot water. Sticking a couple of tea bags and two Styrofoam cups into a paper bag with the box of pancakes, I cleaned up the counter and left the rest of the pancakes for the others.

When I arrived at the park, I almost expected Elian to waiting for me in our spot, but it was empty.

"Hey, Elian!" I called as I settled on the log, placing the paper bag and tumbler beside me. "I brought pancakes. I thought we could have breakfast together?" I asked hopefully, scanning the trees for some sign of him.

After last night, or early this morning, I'd thought we were over this hurdle. Elian had sat with me in his true form, and

I'd taken that to mean he was finally comfortable around me. Had I been wrong?

"It's okay if you don't want to," I said, trying my best to hide my disappointment. This was my fault. I'd promised Elian I'd be patient, and yet I was being anything but.

"How about this? The tea and pancakes are hot, and I want you to try them that way. I'll go and get you a phone like we talked about yesterday, and you can eat in peace. I'll come back in thirty minutes."

I waited for some kind of reaction from Elian, but when nothing happened, I poured some water into a cup, dropped in a tea bag, and placed it beside the open box of pancakes.

"All right, leaving these for you here," I said before quickly making my way to the exit.

After a quick trip to TOSS, I returned to the park to find the pancakes and tea gone. Elian had even packed everything up.

I smiled when I spotted the word Yummy spelled out in pebbles on the log, along with a small stack of strawberries. Sitting beside it, I ran my fingertip along the pebbles before scanning my surroundings.

"I'm glad you liked it. I can make a different flavors for you another day. Berries, maybe?" I mused as I popped a juicy strawberry into my mouth, knowing how much he liked all things berries.

Throughout the day, there were a few times when I thought Elian might show up, but he never did. I tried not to feel too disappointed by it, but try as I might, I couldn't quite control my feelings, and I was worried Elian could sense them. The last thing I wanted to do was rush him or, worse, push him too far.

By the time evening arrived, I was full of strawberries and feeling much better than earlier in the day. I'd stopped obsessing over Elian's reluctance to show and accepted the fact that

I needed to be patient. I'd promised Elian—and myself—that I would be, and I wasn't going to break my promise.

"I'm sorry about earlier, Elian," I said, and I was almost sure I heard him move around in the trees. The sun had set a few minutes ago, and the clearing was dark enough that I couldn't see past the first line of trees. I wondered if he was watching me, and I hoped that if he was, he could see the sincerity on my face. "I'm sorry if I was being pushy. The last thing I ever wanted to do was pressure you. I promise you I can wait. Take all the time you need, okay? I'll be right here."

As expected, there was no reply. Smiling to myself, I grabbed the phone I'd bought for Elian earlier today. I spent the next ten minutes explaining how the device worked as well as how Elian could charge it using the solar charger. I had no idea if Elian understood a word of what I'd said, but I hoped he had. I liked the idea of being able to stay in contact with him when I wasn't here, and who knew? Maybe Elian would enjoy talking on the phone.

"I'll leave this here for you. Make sure you keep it somewhere dry, okay? Water is really bad for electronics," I said, and then wondered if it was too much. I had no idea how much Elian knew about modern appliances, but the last thing I wanted was to sound condescending. Elian deserved better than that.

"Okay, I'm going to stop dragging my feet now and just go home. I'll see you tomorrow, Elian. Have a good night," I said, and an owl hoot was my only reply. I wondered if it was just a normal owl or if April was making one of her rounds. She was a protective familiar, just like her mage Cassian was, and I knew she looked out for the whole town too.

Shaking my head, I packed up the trash from the phone packaging as well as the breakfast. With a last glance at the clearing around me, I got to my feet and started heading toward the exit.

Just as I stepped through the trees, I felt something brush against my arm. It was a tree branch but not quite. Elian?

I smiled as I glanced around me, almost able to sense him. "Sweet dreams, Elian."

My heart felt a hundred times lighter as I made my way toward the exit, and I breathed in the night air as I walked through the streets of Mistvale, soaking in the slight chill that surrounded me.

Today hadn't gone the way I'd hoped it would, but it'd still been a good day.

Elian

After Alden left, I stepped into the clearing and picked up the phone and charger he'd left me. I quickly realized that my fingers didn't work on the screen the way Alden's had. The screen was made for human touch, so I shifted into my human form before trying again.

I smiled when the screen finally reacted. Squinting against the bright light it emitted, I clicked around as I tried to familiarize myself with the device. Luckily, everything was labeled neatly, so it wasn't too difficult to find a list of contacts.

The list was small, and Alden's name was right at the top with a star next to it. Other than him, I also had his friends' numbers. I didn't think I'd need to contact any of them, but I supposed it was good to have in case I couldn't get hold of Alden.

I wasn't sure how long I spent messing with the phone, but I quickly realized why humans were so obsessed with the damned thing-. Of course, as soon as I realized that I promptly put the device away. I made sure to keep it and the charger in a dry nook in my private garden, someplace I knew the rain couldn't reach.

Sunrise was still a few hours away, and I didn't feel like sleeping. The events of today kept replaying in my mind on repeat, and I couldn't get over how much I'd disappointed Alden.

He'd promised to be patient, and he *was* patient. I didn't think anyone else would've waited as easily as he was waiting for me. Yesterday, I'd approached him because I'd been worried about him, because I'd been so relieved to see he was okay that I hadn't been able to control myself. And yet I'd chickened out this morning.

Maybe I'd feel better if I could figure out exactly why I was so resistant to the idea of revealing myself to Alden. I knew he wouldn't mock me. Maybe I was just afraid of not being what he wanted, what he needed.

Alden and I were mates, which logically implied that I was what he needed—and vice versa. Yet my mind didn't care for the logic at all. It was intent on driving me mad with anxiety, and I was powerless against it.

Maybe some distance would be helpful. Alden visited me every day, and it wasn't fair to make him have a one-sided conversation day after day. Surely he had better things to do than sit here all day in the hope that I would join him.

Alden had friends, a family. He had other people who weren't afraid to spend time with him. He could spend his time in so many ways that were better than hanging out in this park all on his own.

Even though Alden knew I was around, there were only so many one-sided conversations he would be able to handle. Knowing what I knew of him, I knew he wouldn't give up, no matter how miserable waiting made him. He'd promised me patience, and he was going to be patient, even if it killed him.

I couldn't have that. I couldn't allow Alden to hurt himself in an attempt to help me. A little space might be the best idea. For both of us.

Alden could use the time to focus on his family, and I could use it to work through my thoughts and finally gather up the courage to face him. It would be a win-win.

Of course, I hated the idea of not seeing Alden every day after weeks of hanging out, but this was the best course of action for everyone involved. Alden had put his life on hold for me long enough.

Decision made, I closed my eyes and spread my focus throughout my land, filling it with my magic and convincing it to not allow anyone—human or supe—to step foot inside. In all my years, I'd never completely cut others off from my park, but it seemed like the right thing to do now. I didn't want to cut off just Alden, and I had a feeling his friends would try to approach me if they realized I'd hurt their friend. I didn't *want* to hurt Alden, but I knew forcing him to stay away would. It was the best thing to do, though. For both of us. It would help in the long run.

I felt like my thoughts were going round and round in circles, so I decided to take a small nap after all, if only to quiet my mind. Sleeping already wasn't my forte, and it was even harder to fall asleep now when my thoughts were filled with worry about Alden and me. I didn't want to mess things up between us—not that there was much between us at the moment to mess—but I had a feeling I was about to do exactly that. Yet I couldn't think of a better alternative. I couldn't keep tugging Alden along the way I had for the last few weeks. He deserved better.

Closing my eyes, I forced myself to breathe evenly as I lay on the ground in my garden. Usually, I would've slipped into one of the trees to sleep, but since I'd blocked off the park, there was no danger of anyone walking up to me, and I could just be.

A soft, cool breeze wafted over me, and I opened my eyes to stare up at the twinkling stars. It had been a while since I'd done this. My fingers twitched against the ground underneath, and I wished Alden was here. I wanted him beside me, our arms pressed together, our fingers linked as we both gazed at the sky, at the millions of stars that were much older than both of us combined.

I fell asleep imagining the scenario, and then my dreams brought Alden back to me. In my dream, I wasn't afraid of showing myself. Instead, I hugged him the way I had before, and this time, I didn't let go.

EIGHT

Alden

I hummed under my breath as I strolled toward the park. I'd slept in today, and I felt well-rested and ready to tackle the day. It didn't hurt that the weather was perfect today either. Of course, that could change at the drop of a hat in Mistvale, but I'd learned to appreciate the sun and the rain equally. They both had their charms, after all, and as long as I had a shelter for the rain, I loved it.

Since I'd woken up late, I'd skipped making breakfast and instead picked up a few cupcakes from the bakery. I'd been hoping to make something for Elian, but I didn't want to be too late.

I smiled as the park entrance came into view, my thoughts returning to Elian and what I'd tell him about today. Contrary to what I'd thought at first, I actually really enjoyed talking to Elian. There was something strangely freeing about knowing that Elian was listening but wouldn't interrupt, and I'd told him things it had taken me decades to share with my friends.

I was so lost in thought as I walked that it took me a moment to realize something was wrong. Stopping in my tracks, I glanced around and realized I was on my way back home. What the fuck?

Turning around, I started walking toward the park, this time conscious of my every step. The need to stop and turn around, to leave, grew with every step, and I was so surprised it took me a moment to realize what was happening. This was Elian's magic at work. But why was it shoving me away? As far as I knew, it was only supposed to work on humans.

Pushing against the growing unease, I walked closer and closer to the park, but I couldn't force myself to cross the threshold.

"Elian!" I called out, but as was the norm, there was no reply. What the hell was going on? Why had Elian barred my entrance to the park? Had I done something wrong?

I thought back to yesterday and wondered if my apology hadn't been enough. I'd pushed Elian to show himself, and then I'd acted like a jackass when he didn't. Was that what had made Elian pull away?

Unlocking my phone, I found Elian's contact and pulled up a blank text chain. I wasn't even sure if he'd tried to use the phone or if he'd merely stuck it in some corner. Still, it was the only thing I could think to try.

Me: Hey, Elian. Are you okay? If this is about yesterday, I'm truly sorry I pushed you. That was not my intention at all. If you need some time, just let me know, and I'll leave. I promise.

Sending the message, I held my breath and waited. Would he even reply? Had he figured out the whole texting thing? I'd told him about it yesterday, even demonstrated how it worked on his phone, but I had no idea if he'd actually seen it.

After about five minutes, my phone pinged, and I almost dropped the paper bag of cupcakes in my haste to unlock my phone.

Elian: I'm sorry. I just need a little time. To myself.

I stared at the message with a frown, not quite sure what to make of it. So this was because of yesterday. Elian hadn't denied that. Maybe he'd decided I wasn't worth the effort of changing his whole way of living? Or maybe he needed the time to make that decision.

Elian: This isn't your fault, Alden. I just need to figure some things out.

Shaking my head at the message, I took a deep breath and thumbed a quick reply.

Me: Okay. Can I text you sometimes? Just to check in?

I realized as I waited for his reply that Elian was taking so long because he wasn't in the habit of using a phone. I imagined him—in a faceless human body because I had no idea what his human form looked like—using his index finger to type each letter, and the image made me chuckle. Shaking my head at myself, I stared at my phone and waited for his reply, completely rooted to the spot.

Elian: I'd like that. I will text you too, if that's okay.

Me: Of course! Maybe we can even talk through texts. If you want, that is. Or I can leave you alone.

Elian: That sounds good. You'll have to forgive me, though. It seems I can't type very fast.

I smiled at his reply, almost able to imagine his blushing cheeks as he wrote that message.

Me: That's okay. I don't mind waiting, remember? I brought cupcakes for you. Should I leave them out here?

Elian: Yes please.

I chuckled at the speed of his reply, then carefully folded the end of the bag so it wouldn't open on its own before leaning forward and dropping it inside the park. Elian's magic pushed at me, and I breathed it in before slowly taking a step back.

Me: Eat them quickly. They're your favorite flavor. I'm leaving now. You can text me whenever you want, okay?

Elian: Okay. Thank you.

Me: There's no need to thank me, Elian. I didn't do anything.

Elian: You understood me, and respected my wishes. So thank you.

Me: My pleasure. I'm leaving now, I swear.

Elian: Okay. Bye, Alden.

Me: Bye, Elian. I hope you figure things out.

The walk back home was nothing like before. The sun didn't feel as bright and cheerful anymore, and a part of me hoped it would start raining. Raiden was a lucky bastard. He could change the whole freaking weather with his emotions, but unfortunately, I was nowhere near as powerful.

My gut magic did tell me I was doing the right thing, though, which I guessed I should take some comfort in. My magic had never led me wrong, and I had no reason to doubt it now. Well, except for how shitty the idea of not being around Elian for an unknown amount of time made me feel.

Hopefully, Elian would work out whatever he needed to soon because after weeks of spending every day with him, I didn't know how long I could go without 'seeing' him.

Elian

The cupcakes were delicious as always, and yet they felt like ash in my mouth. I hated that I'd made Alden leave. I hated that I'd hurt him, and yet I couldn't deny the feeling that it was the right thing to do.

At first, I'd thought that if Alden was here every day, I would slowly get over whatever was holding me back, but instead,

I'd just gotten used to our one-sided conversations. Sure, I'd shown him my true form and even talked to him when he was in his unicorn form, but there had still been a wall between us, a wall that I couldn't seem to break through no matter how hard I tried.

I couldn't go on like this, though. I couldn't keep leading Alden on. He was my mate, and he deserved more than that. I needed to do better, and for that, I first needed to understand exactly what was holding me back.

It had been a long, long time since I'd interacted with people. The last time I'd befriended someone had been eight, maybe nine hundred years ago. Back then, Mistvale had been nothing but a forest with a tiny little hamlet built on its edge. I'd been the keeper of the forest, and I'd been determined to keep the humans and supes out of my space.

That was, until one of them befriended me. I'd been a naive fool back then, and I'd fallen for his charms. I hadn't been in love with him or anything, but I'd considered him to be a friend. I'd allowed him and his family into my forest, let them build a house.

Then, I'd woken up one day and found he'd poisoned my trees while I slept with a potion he'd acquired from some witch. In one night, I'd lost half my forest—half my strength and magic.

After that, I'd closed myself off, literally and figuratively. I didn't come out of my trees during the day, and for years, I hadn't allowed anyone into what remained of my forest.

Over the years, my forest became the Silent Creek Park, and I'd slowly started allowing select supes in. I kept an eye on them whenever they were here, though, and I never, ever slept when someone was in my park. I'd learned my lesson, and I didn't plan on failing again.

Was that why I was so reluctant to show myself to Alden? Because I was worried he'd betray me too?

But Alden was nothing like that greedy human. He was a unicorn, the last of his kind. More importantly, he was my mate. If I couldn't trust my mate, I had absolutely no hope of being able to trust anyone.

It wasn't just that, though. I was also worried that I...that I wouldn't be enough. I didn't know if I would ever be brave enough to leave my park. I knew how much Alden loved his family, and the last thing I wanted to do was come between them or make Alden choose between us. But if I couldn't get myself together, that was exactly what Alden would have to do. I didn't want that for him.

Which meant things needed to change. I needed to change. Not for Alden—okay, maybe a little for him—but because I wanted to. I wanted to change so I could be with Alden without any guilt. I wanted to feel worthy of being Alden's mate.

Figuring out how was going to be tough. If only there was someone I could talk to. Alden was out of question, but then who else could I talk to? I didn't know any of the other supes in this town, and it wasn't like I was going to go strolling through the streets looking for them even if I did.

Sighing, I reached for the last cupcake I'd been saving, and that was when I saw it. The phone Alden had given me. He'd saved other numbers in it, hadn't he? His friends'? Would it be in bad form if I texted one of them and asked for their assistance?

You can text or call any of them if you ever need anything or can't reach me. Just tell them who you are, and they'll jump at the chance to help, Alden's voice echoed in my head, and I stared at the phone as I took a bite of the strawberry cupcake. Maybe asking for help wouldn't be a complete disaster. I'd heard so much about Alden's friends. It would be nice to get to know one of them.

Once I'd finished the cupcake, I wiped my hands on my pants—one of the perks of my magic was being able to keep the clothes when I shifted to my human form—and picked up the phone.

Opening the contacts list, I scrolled through the listed names and tried to remember what Alden had told me about each of them.

Memphis was an incubus with two sons and a griffin mate. He was also the only one who knew I was Alden's mate.

Quill was a wolf shifter and mated to a werewolf and a human. Alden hadn't told him about me because his human mate's brother was mated to one of the biggest gossips in town, and Alden had been worried he'd spread the news and I would have a horde of supe visitors because of it.

Vo was a gargoyle, a protective and patient man mated to a human. He was also currently busy keeping his mate and his new daughter safe from a stalker, so he was out of the question.

Memphis was clearly the obvious choice, but I was worried asking him for help would put him in a tough spot with Alden.

I blinked when I realized I'd missed one of the names: Orion. He was Memphis's mate, and while he was Alden's friend too, I was sure they weren't as close as the other three.

Maybe the griffin could help me. After all, everything Alden had told me about him said he was a warm and caring man, and from what I'd gathered, he'd been a bit of a loner before he met Memphis too. He might just be the perfect person to help me get out of my shell. Now all I needed to do was send him a message.

NINE

Alden

It'd been a week since I went to the park. Elian and I had texted almost every day, but it just wasn't the same. I missed the park. I missed being surrounded by Elian's aura. I missed Elian.

I was going to be good, though. He'd asked me for time, and I intended to give it to him. I didn't care how long it took—well, I cared, but I wouldn't let it change my mind or do something that could damage what we'd built so far, fragile as it was.

The one good thing that had happened this past week was that Vo, Trick, and Lena were finally free of the asshole who'd been stalking them. I was relieved for Vo, and happy too. He could finally start building a life with his mate and kid without having to look over his shoulder. He deserved all the good in the world, and I was glad he'd found Trick and Lena. They completed him in a way our little family never could've, and I loved seeing the joy on his face whenever he was with them.

Vo had also officially moved out of the house, which meant now it was just me, Memphis, Orion, and the boys. I wondered if some day I might move out too, and if so, where I would go. Neither Memphis nor Orion had asked me to move out, and

I knew they never would. I was the fun uncle they could leave Neel and Pax with when they wanted to go out for date nights, and neither of them wanted to give that up. Honestly, I loved spending time with Neel and Pax, so I had no problem with our current arrangement, but I couldn't help daydreaming about it.

Maybe someday I would move into the park with Elian. I didn't even know if he had a house in there, but if not I could just live in my true form. I honestly didn't care as long as I got to be with him.

"Alden, I need your help," Memphis declared as he flew into the room, and I raised my brows up at him as I adjusted my glasses. I didn't wear them all the time since they were mostly for show, but I liked having a barrier when I was feeling down, and that was definitely the case at the moment.

"What's up?" I asked Memphis as he took the stool beside mine and turned it to face me.

"I know you're moping right now because you can't see Elian, but this is urgent. And possibly life-threatening," he added, and I blinked. I knew Memphis well enough to not trust a word he was saying, but at the same time, I couldn't ignore it completely, not when there was a possibility that even half of what he was saying was true.

"Explain," I said, ignoring the comment about me moping. It was true enough, and I didn't want to give him any fuel.

"It's Orion. He's been texting with someone," Memphis said, and I raised a brow at him.

"And that's a problem why?" I asked, making him huff. His black curls bounced with the movement, and I shook my head at his crazy dramatics.

"Because I don't know who he's talking to. I don't think it's anyone in our group or even the clan," he said in a hushed whisper, and I blinked when I realized he was honestly worried.

"What are you worried about, exactly? You think Orion's cheating on you?" I asked dubiously, and Memphis's eyes widened.

"Of course not! I'd never think that! Don't be stupid, Alden."

"Then what exactly are you worried about? It's not a crime to talk to someone outside the clan. Maybe he made a new friend at the library," I suggested, and Memphis sighed.

"Maybe. But Orion won't tell me anything about him. All he'll say is he's a friend of a friend and needs his help," he said, tapping his nails on the counter as he stared at it, as if the answers would be revealed if he stared long enough.

"Maybe you should let it go. Orion will tell you when he's ready to. The friend of a friend probably asked him to keep the secret. You know Orion wouldn't hide things from you unless he had to," I said, and Memphis smiled.

"You're right. You always are. And don't worry—Elian will invite you back soon. He's probably just overwhelmed. It must be weird to go from not talking to anyone for decades to having someone who wants to spend so much time with you. Give him time. You'll be fine," Memphis said as he wrapped his arm around my shoulders and pulled me into a side-hug.

"I know. I just hate waiting," I grumbled, making him snicker.

"I didn't think I'd ever see the day where you would be Mr. Impatient, and yet here we are," he said with a grin, and I smacked his stomach.

"Shut up. I never claimed to be Mr. Patient. That's Vo. I just trust my magic."

"What's it telling you now?" Memphis asked, and I sighed.

"To tell you that whoever Orion's talking to means him no harm," I said, and he smiled widely.

"That's great, and I am really glad to hear that, but I meant what is it telling you about your situation?"

"That I should wait," I grumbled, making him chuckle.

"You know what? We need a day out. I'm going to text Vo and Quill, and the four of us are going to do something together. Maybe a swim in the Creek?" Memphis said, and I raised a brow at him.

"A swim?"

"Yeah, it'll be fun! Come on! Just the four of us, like old times," he said, shaking me with each word as if it would make me agree more easily.

"All right, all right. If the others are up for it, let's do it," I said. It had been a while since the four of us hung out on our own. Usually, the guys' mates joined us, or we were with the whole clan.

I wouldn't admit it out loud, but I missed my friends. It would be good to spend some time with them.

Elian

Orion: Memphis keeps asking me who I'm talking to. I don't know why he's worried, but it's adorable to watch.

Me: I'm sorry. I didn't mean to cause trouble for you. You can tell him if you want.

Orion: Are you kidding? No way. This is fun.

Me: As you wish. I'm really grateful for your help.

Orion: It's no problem. You're Alden's mate, which means you're family. I'm happy to help however I can.

Me: Maybe you could come to the park one of these days? I would like to try talking to you face-to-face in my human form.

As practice. I haven't been able to do it with Alden, and I want to change that.

Orion didn't reply instantly, and I wondered if that had been too much. Texting with me was one thing, but coming all the way to the park—not that I had any idea how far he lived—was a whole another deal. I didn't want to cause any trouble for Orion.

Orion: Sorry about that. Memphis and the others are going for a swim. I'd love to come to the park if you're up to it. Maybe in an hour?

I blinked, surprised he wanted to so quickly. My question had been more along the lines of 'maybe someday,' but what was the point of waiting? The longer I waited, the longer Alden would have to stay away, and neither of us wanted that.

Me: An hour sounds good.

Orion: Great. The boys are at school, so I can leave as soon as Memphis and Alden do. I'm looking forward to meeting you, Elian.

Me: Me too.

I was also scared to death, but of course I wasn't going to say that to Orion. He'd been a good friend the past few days, and he was surprisingly easy to talk to. It was why I'd decided to give meeting him a shot so quickly. I was worried that if I didn't push myself, I'd end up getting stuck in yet another loop.

The next hour was the slowest sixty minutes of my life, and I spent it in my human form trying to decide if my appearance looked fine. I'd been so very cut off from the human world for so long that I had lost all sense of fashion and current trends. The visitors of the park gave me some ideas, but it wasn't like I could venture out to do some shopping. The clothes I now wore were perfect in condition, but they were also more than five hundred years old.

I sensed Orion step into the park, and a burst of anxiety almost knocked me onto my ass. He was here. This was really happening.

Taking a deep breath, I stepped out of the trees and made my way to where I could sense he was, just off the path near the entrance.

"Orion," I greeted when I could finally see him, and he smiled widely.

"Elian! It's so good to meet you," he said, and I ducked my head in a nod.

"Thank you for coming," I said, then shook my head. "And also for helping me."

"Of course. It's my pleasure, trust me. It's been fun," he assured me, and the grin on his face told me he meant it.

"Come on. I have a spot we can sit in," I said, and led him to a different clearing than the one Alden and I shared. That one was just ours. No one else was allowed to go there.

Orion followed me as I pushed through the trees, taking a path only I could see. I knew every inch of this park like the back of my hand.

"Here we are," I said, waving Orion toward the stump of a tree. It'd fallen during a bad storm, and I'd smoothed the remaining stump to make it into a place someone could sit.

Orion blinked before taking a seat, and I folded myself on the ground in front of him.

"Oh, you should sit here," Orion started to protest, but I waved him off.

"Don't worry. This is my home. I can sit anywhere," I said with a smile, patting the ground below me.

Orion still looked dismayed, but he didn't push the issue. Instead, his eyes roamed around before coming back to me. "Your park is really beautiful. You should be proud of it."

Warmth filled my chest at his praise, and I smiled widely. I was proud of my park. It'd survived through so much and kept flourishing regardless of how many people tried to stop it. I was proud of every tree, every sliver of grass, every weed, and every bug and animal in here.

"Thank you," I said, and Orion smiled. Then, I asked the question that had been brewing in the back of my mind since Orion arrived. "How's Alden?"

While Alden and I had texted every day since I asked for some space, it wasn't the same as seeing his face and hearing his voice. I had no idea if the messages he sent were true, if he was doing as well as he'd said he was.

"He's okay. A little mopey, but fine mostly. Memphis, Quill, and Vo took him out today to take his mind off things," he said, and I pursed my lips. *Off you*, was what he actually meant.

"Does this mean the others know about me?" I asked curiously. I knew Alden's reasoning behind not telling everyone, and I was partly grateful for it. But I also didn't want to make Alden keep secrets from the people he was closest to for my sake. It wasn't fair to him.

"No, they don't. Memphis is the one who planned everything, and I'm sure he gave the others a different reason for it," Orion said with a reassuring smile, but for some reason, it only made me feel worse.

"Could you give me a minute, please?" I asked as I stood up, and Orion's brows furrowed as he nodded.

Quickly, I rushed toward my garden and dug my phone out of its hiding spot. There were no new messages, so I pulled up my last message to Alden and typed up another one.

Me: Hey, Alden. Just wanted to say that you can tell your friends about me if you need to talk to them. I don't mind. I promise.

I waited a minute, but when there was no reply, I returned the phone to its spot before making my way back to Orion. Hopefully, Alden's friends would prove as helpful to him as Orion was being to me.

TEN

Alden

Elian: Hey, Alden. Just wanted to say that you can tell your friends about me if you need to talk to them. I don't mind. I promise.

I stared at Elian's text for three whole minutes before Quill made me put my phone away. While Elian had never asked to keep him a secret, my gut had told me telling the others would be a bad idea, that they might end up scaring him off. But now Elian had given me permission himself, and I didn't know what to do.

While on one hand I hated keeping secrets from my friends—my family, really—on the other hand I knew exactly what they'd do if they knew. Quill would be at the park within the hour, curious about the man I was mated to. Honestly, he should've been a cat shifter with how curious he was.

Vo would probably go all protective and want to meet Elian simply so he could ascertain he wasn't a threat. While he usually took my word for it and believed my gut, I had a feeling in this instance he would insist on double-checking.

If Memphis hadn't already known, he would've been the one I would be the most worried about, but he'd been surprisingly good at keeping things quiet.

I choose to not make a decision for now. After all, this outing was supposed to be about taking my mind off Elian, and telling my friends about him would just end up doing the opposite. No, it was better to leave it be for now. Maybe once I could see Elian again, I would tell them.

"What are you thinking about so deeply over there?" Vo asked, and I smiled at him.

"Nothing, nothing," I said, waving him off. He raised a brow at me because he knew me too well, but Memphis cut in before he could ask me another question.

"Come on! Are we going to swim or what?" he asked, and Vo shook his head before grabbing Memphis by the shoulders and dragging him toward the edge of the creek.

Memphis shrieked, and Quill and I burst into laughter as Vo bodily threw him into the water, clothes and everything.

"You bastard!" Memphis sputtered as his head burst out while Vo bent over with laughter.

I glanced over at Quill and he winked before quietly approaching Vo using all his wolf shifter soft-footedness.

Of course, sneaking up on a gargoyle who worked as a bodyguard wasn't easy—or maybe even impossible—and between one second and the next, Vo had turned around, grabbed Quill around the waist, and thrown him into the water, sending both him and Memphis under.

I took an automatic step back and raised my palms in surrender when he turned to me, and Vo grinned before turning around and leaping in just as the other two surfaced.

Taking my time, I slowly walked toward the edge while the three tried to get one over on each other. Sometimes being the oldest—and therefore the one who needed to be responsible—one sucked.

"Oh, hey, guys!" a new voice called, and I scanned the water to spot a head of silver hair...and a merman's tail.

"Jules! What are you doing here?" Memphis called, and Jules quirked a brow at him before swimming closer.

"Well, let's see. I'm a merman-siren mated to a dolphin shifter. Whatever could I possibly be doing in water?" he asked, widening his eyes in mock-innocence.

A squeak from the water made him roll his eyes, and he glanced down where I assumed Firey, his mate, was. "I'm not being a dick."

"What I meant was," Memphis interrupted another round of chirps from Firey, "what are you doing out here in the open? There are still humans in the town."

"We'd never risk exposure," Jules said, sounding offended by the thought. "Rhiannon did a spell on us so human eyes would slide right past us. Which means that if some human comes this way, they'll think you're talking to yourself."

I shook my head at the absolute glee in Jules's voice. I used to think he was one of the sane ones, but it looked like I was mistaken.

"What are you guys doing here?" Jules asked, and I fielded the question before Memphis could give a sassy answer that would probably devolve this conversation even more than it already had.

"Just hanging out," I said, and Quill jumped in.

"Yeah, with Vo being busy protecting his mate and Alden and his new...hobby, we haven't really been able to spend much time together," he said, and I tried not to react at the way he'd said it. Did he know about Elian?

My eyes slid to Memphis, and he gave a small shake of his head. He hadn't said anything. Maybe Quill was just guessing, trying to get me to give a reaction.

"Oh, okay. Well, we'll leave you guys to it and find somewhere more... private," Jules said before glancing into the water. "Race you!"

Jules dived into the water and then disappeared in a streak of silver and greenish-blue. I assumed Firey had chased after him and turned my focus to my friends.

"If you could be any other supe, what would you be?" Quill asked as I finally slipped into the water like a normal person. "I'd be a merman. They're so pretty."

"Do Joy and Tate know you think Jules is pretty?" Memphis asked with a raised brow, and Quill splashed water on his face in reply.

"Of course they do," he shot back, before turning to me. "Come on, Alden. Tell me. What supe would you be?"

"Alden's a fucking *unicorn*. If I was a unicorn, I would not want to change," Vo said, and I rolled my eyes.

"Yeah, I don't think you'd feel the same way if you actually were one. I think I'd like to be some kind of bird shifter. I've always wondered what flying feels like," I said, and Quill hummed thoughtfully.

"I'd be a dragon. A fire dragon," Memphis said, and I raised a brow at him.

"You'd have to fight Raiden for territory then," Vo said, and Memphis shrugged.

"I could take him."

"Yeah, right," Quill said with a chuckle, and got a face full of water for his amusement. "What about you, Vo? Unicorn?"

"Nah. I like being a gargoyle. I like protecting people, and being able to turn to stone is not a bad power to have."

"That's true," I agreed, glad that at least one of us was completely content with what he was. While I didn't hate being a unicorn, I couldn't deny the fact that if given the choice, I'd have opted to be something different. Life hadn't always been easy, but luckily I'd found some great friends along the way who'd made life a lot more worthwhile.

Elian

The moment Orion left the park, I slid into the closest tree and scattered myself into my land, too overwhelmed by the whole experience to function in any other way. I hadn't spent that much time with another sentient being in a while, not in my human form.

I felt proud of myself for having accomplished it, especially because it meant I was one step closer to seeing Alden again.

I wouldn't invite him back just yet. No. First, I needed some practice. I wanted to be able to spend time with Alden without having to retreat into my trees after a few hours. I didn't want to feel this overwhelmed the whole time. When I was with Alden, I wanted to be completely focused on him.

Still, today had been a good day. It'd shown me that if I pushed myself just a little, I could do it. I could interact with someone without making a complete fool of myself.

Drifting through my land, I patched up any plants that needed some extra support to grow or heal, letting my magic flow through every root, every trunk, giving them health and nourishment. My relationship with the flora on my land was a symbiotic one. My magic kept them healthy and flourishing, and in return, the trees gave me whatever fruits and vegetables I needed.

Once I'd done all I could for the trees, I moved to my private garden and transformed into my true form. I'd been thinking about building something here for Alden. I didn't think he would ever want to leave his nice house with indoor plumbing and everything, but I'd been thinking about building something in case he wanted to stay over for a few days. Maybe I could request some of the trees here to make something...

Settling on the log I used as a bed, I closed my eyes and decided a few hours of sleep might help get the last of the anxiety out of me. I fell asleep to the thoughts of Alden, and then dreamed of sharing my garden with him.

Over the next few weeks, Orion and I spent quite a lot of time together. We mostly talked about inane things, but I learned a lot about Alden's friends from Orion. They were a unique bunch, and I found their dynamic utterly fascinating. I was also glad Alden had such good friends, and from what Alden had told me, I knew he'd been quite lonely before he found them.

One day, Orion brought a few bags of clothes with him. Apparently, my clothes were too old-fashioned, and while I looked cute in them—Orion's words, not mine—he thought I should have some 'current' clothes in case Alden and I wanted to go out sometime.

The thought of venturing out of the park was still scary to me, but that was one milestone I wanted to cross with Alden.

I had a feeling I would find it much easier to do with Alden by my side.

When he'd found out about my love of sweet treats, Orion had insisted on getting some for me, but I'd declined. The sweets were something I shared with Alden, and I wanted to keep it that way. The cupcakes and pastries were what had started our interactions, and I didn't want to share that with anyone else.

After around three weeks since the day Orion first came to the park, I finally felt ready enough to invite Alden back to the park. I'd seen Orion yesterday, and he'd agreed that it was time I called Alden back, that I was as ready as I'd ever be.

With Orion's help, I'd made some preparations in our clearing for Alden, and I was as nervous as I was excited to see his reaction.

The last three weeks had been brutal without Alden after spending almost every day with him before that, but they'd been worth it. I felt more confident now, in myself and in my ability to be myself before Alden. With Orion's help and all that practice, I wasn't scared anymore.

Once everything was ready, I grabbed my phone from its nook and pulled up the messages between Alden and me. We'd talked a lot over the last three weeks, and the phone had kept me from feeling completely cut off from Alden. Maybe not all human inventions were bad.

Me: Hey, Alden. Would you like to come to the park sometime soon?

I paced around the clearing as I waited for his reply, eyeing everything to make sure one last time that nothing more needed to be done. When my phone finally buzzed in my hand, I almost dropped it in my eagerness to see what Alden had said.

Alden: Yes! How about right now?

I blinked, surprised but mostly pleased that Alden wanted to see me as soon as possible too. I'd worried that I was getting a lot more invested in this thing between us, but it was clear Alden was just as eager as me.

Me: Sounds good. See you in our clearing.

ELEVEN

Alden

I couldn't remember the last time I'd raced to be somewhere with this much enthusiasm. Hell, I'd even borrowed Memphis's car because walking would've taken too long. If I wasn't worried about being spotted, I'd have shifted and galloped there.

I'd been helping Pax and Neel with their homework when I'd gotten Elian's text, and I'd had to excuse myself from it. Noel was hosting another one of his lunch parties today, and while I'd been planning to go today, now there was no question where I'd rather go.

Orion hadn't seemed to mind. Actually, he'd pretty much pushed me out of the door and assured me he'd help the kids and tell the others I wouldn't be attending. If I hadn't been so preoccupied with getting to Elian, I might've found it curious.

It didn't take me long to reach the park in the car, and I quickly parked before walking through the entrance. My shoulders relaxed the moment I stepped through the barrier, a little because it'd stopped me the last time I was here, but mostly because being surrounded by Elian's aura always felt pleasant.

My legs took the familiar path to our clearing without an input from my brain, which was probably why I was so shocked when I reached it.

The clearing had transformed. While I could tell it was the same, it had changed so drastically that it looked nothing like its old self.

The edges of the clearing were now lined with bushes upon bushes of colorful flowers. Bursts of reds, yellows, oranges, and purples circled the clearing, and twinkling fairy lights hung from the trees, washing the whole place in a warm, golden glow. The sun had almost set, and with all the trees, there was no other light in the clearing except for the fairy lights. How had he even gotten them to work without electricity?

It was only then, when I'd pulled my eyes away from the flowers and the sparkling lights, that I realized the log I usually sat on was already occupied. The person seated on it had their back to me, and all I could see was a head of greenish-black hair and a slim frame.

Cautiously, I walked deeper into the clearing, and a soft gasp slipped past my lips when the person turned around to face me.

Even though I'd never seen Elian's human form before, I knew without a shadow of doubt it was him. I took a few more steps toward him until I stood right in front of him, and he slowly rose to his feet, his vibrant green eyes wide as they watched me. His skin was a beautiful shade of brown, and the golden light made it seem like he was glowing.

"Elian," I breathed in a soft whisper, and his lips tilted upward in a smile. I brought my arms up for a hug before stopping short, and it was Elian who came closer, who wrapped his arms around my hips and sank into the hug.

He was shorter than me, I realized as I embraced him tightly. The top of his head barely brushed my chin, and I tucked him in tighter, wishing and hoping I'd never have to let go.

"I missed you," I whispered, not at all caring if it made me sound a bit lovesick.

"I missed you too. I'm sorry I made you wait so long," he replied, his words getting muffled in my shirt. Neither of us pulled away, though.

"It was worth it," I assured him, and we held each other for another few minutes before Elian finally pulled away.

Dropping my arms to my sides, I took another good look at the clearing before meeting Elian's eyes. "Did you do all this?"

"Most of it," he agreed, scuffing his shoes in the dirt.

"This should've probably been the first thing I said, but Elian...you're beautiful," I said, and his eyes shot to mine, wide as saucers. "I mean it," I insisted when he kept staring at me, and he glanced away, his eyes roaming everywhere without settling.

"How are the lights working? I didn't think you had electricity here," I said in an attempt to change the subject. Elian clearly didn't know what to do with the compliment, and I decided to be subtler in my approach next time. I didn't want to scare him off now that he was finally ready to spend time with me.

"They're battery-powered," he said, and I nodded. Of course. Wait...had he gone shopping then?

Reaching out, careful to project my movements, I took Elian's hand in mine and tugged him toward the log. Once we were both seated, I turned so I could face him. Elian didn't try to pull his hand away, so I kept a hold of it, slowly running my thumb over his smooth skin. It was interesting how different his skin felt in this form, but then again, I grew fur in my other form, so who was I to talk?

"I'm so glad you texted me," I said after a moment, and Elian smiled at me.

"Me too. I was worried that I might've taken too long."

Meeting his eyes, I squeezed his hand and said, "Never. I promised you patience, Elian, and I would've waited as long as you needed. I've lived a long life, and I've learned to be patient. Living with Memphis, Quill, and Vo was a far worse test of my tolerance than this," I added with a grin, and Elian chuckled softly. The sound went straight to my chest and lit it up from the inside, and I promised myself I'd keep finding ways to make Elian laugh.

"I don't think they're as bad as you make them sound," Elian said, and I shrugged. "Hopefully, I'll meet them soon, and then I can come to my own conclusions."

The thought of my friends meeting Elian filled me with warmth, and I nodded quickly. I wouldn't push Elian to meet them, but the day he said he was ready, I'd bring them right over.

"Oh, I collected these for you," Elian said after a moment, then reached behind the log to pull out a woven basket full of a variety of fruits.

"Oh damn, I missed these. You realize you've completely ruined me for any others, right? The other day, Memphis gave me a store-bought apple, and I couldn't eat it after the first bite," I complained as I picked up a strawberry and popped it into my mouth, and Elian laughed again.

"I'm sorry?" he said questioningly, and I rolled my eyes.

"Just promise me you'll keep feeding me, and we'll be good," I said, and he smiled.

"I vow to keep feeding you the sweetest and juiciest of fruits, Alden," Elian said, and I grinned widely.

Pushing my glasses up, I sifted through the fruits before pulling out a blueberry and offering it to Elian. Instead of taking it off my hand, he wrapped his lips around the berry, and I blinked at him as my brain went kaput.

While I gathered myself, Elian happily ate the berry. Had he not realized how...intimate that moment was? Had he not meant it that way? Looking at him, I didn't think he had.

It made me realize that I needed to have that conversation with Elian. He'd been so brave and pushed outside his comfort zone to be able to do this with me. I needed to do the same.

My gut told me it was the right thing to do too, which definitely helped. It didn't mean I wasn't still scared of the prospect, but it made my resolve a little bit stronger.

Elian

Alden was nervous, I realized after he'd been here for about an hour. It was a strange thought, since he was always the more confident one out of the two of us. But something was on his mind.

"Are you okay?" I asked after he'd fidgeted for the thousandth time, and his lavender gaze snapped to mine.

"I'm fine," he said quickly, and then gave a loud sigh. "Actually, there's something I wanted to talk to you about."

"Oh?" I asked, curious and a little bit worried about what it was. If it had him this anxious, it had to be something serious, right?

"It's nothing bad," he assured me, squeezing my hand and reminding me he was still holding it.

"Okay," I said, and then waited for him to continue.

"Well, we haven't really talked about the fact that we're mates," Alden started, and I nodded slowly. We hadn't. After the first time I'd touched him with both of us in our true forms, we hadn't really brought up the topic again. He'd seemed happy that we were mates back then. Had he changed his mind?

"We haven't," I agreed cautiously, worried where he was going with this.

"Well, there's something about me you should know, and I don't know if it changes things for you, but I'd understand if it does," he said, and my brows furrowed. Why would it change things for me?

Alden took a deep breath, and I placed my other hand on top of his. He smiled at me softly and then nodded, as if he'd come to some conclusion. "I'm asexual," he said, and I blinked at him.

"Um, I'm not sure what that means. Sorry," I said, ducking my head. While I understood what the word meant, I didn't comprehend its implications here, and I didn't want to misunderstand anything.

"It's okay. You don't need to apologize. An asexual person is someone who doesn't or rarely feels sexual attraction. It's different for everybody, but for me, it just means I have no interest in sex," Alden explained, and I nodded. That made sense to me.

"I...I think I feel the same," I said.

"You do?" Alden asked, and I nodded.

"I've never had any kind of curiosity about all of that. I thought that was normal," I said with a wry smile.

"It *is* normal," Alden said. "There's just fewer of us and more allosexual people."

"I suppose that's true," I said, then tilted my head questioningly. "Is that what you wanted to tell me?"

"Yeah. I haven't had many long-term relationships, and the ones I had usually ended because my partners needed sex. I didn't blame them, but it made me a little gun-shy. You're my mate, so I was even more worried."

"Well, you have nothing to worry about. Even if I had been, I doubt I would've been more interested in it than you."

Alden smiled and then lowered his head, and I realized this was the first time I was seeing him embarrassed. He was cute when he blushed.

"Do you feel better now?" I asked, and he raised his head, a smile already on his face.

"I do, yeah. I've been wanting to tell you that for a while now, but I couldn't quite gather up the courage. But then you did all of this for me, stepped out of your comfort zone and everything. It made me realize I needed to be brave too," Alden said, and I smiled.

"I did it for both of us," I said, and Alden nodded in acceptance. "And I had help," I added, and he raised a brow.

"You did?"

"Yeah. Turns out phones can be useful sometimes. I befriended Orion, and he's been helping me push myself," I explained, and Alden blinked, apparently surprised. I hadn't asked Orion if he'd told Alden or anyone else, but from Alden's reaction, I presumed he hadn't.

"So you've met Orion then?" Alden asked, and I nodded.

"He's the one who got the lights for me. And these clothes," I explained, waving at my attire of a hooded sweatshirt—which I might have been a little in love with—and jeans. I didn't know why humans insisted on wearing pants so constricting, but I had to admit they looked good.

"I'm glad you became friends with him then," Alden said with a smile, and it looked like he meant it. I'd been worried when I first messaged Orion that I was crossing some kind of unnamed line by contacting one of Alden's friends out of the blue, but since neither of them minded, I hoped it'd been okay.

"I don't think I'm ready yet to leave the park, but this is progress, right?"

Alden smiled and shifted closer to me on the log until our knees brushed. "This is major progress, Elian. I'm proud of you. You don't have to leave the park if you don't want to, of course. I'd never ask you to do that."

"I know," I answered. I wanted to do this for myself. I'd hidden away for far too long, and now that I finally had a reason to explore the world outside my land, I wanted to try.

TWELVE

Alden

"There's something I need to tell you," I said, and the room went quiet all at once.

Vo and Quill watched me with a hundred percent focus, while Memphis rolled his eyes at them. He knew exactly what I was about to tell them, of course, and he wasn't going to hide it, the bastard.

"Oh my God. This is it, isn't it? You're going to tell us the park secret," Quill said, shifting to the edge of the couch in his eagerness.

"Yeah, I am," I said, and he made a squeaking sound that was hilarious if not completely dramatic. These idiots had turned something simple into such a huge deal.

"Oh, cut them some slack, Alden. Tell them before they break," Memphis said, and both their eyes snapped to him.

"You know what he's hiding?"

Memphis grinned. "Perks of living in the same house, I suppose."

"Hey! I *just* moved out," Vo complained, and while that was technically true, we all knew he'd been living with Trick for a lot longer than that.

"Okay, everyone shut the fuck up. Alden, start talking," Quill ordered, and I rolled my eyes.

"I met my mate," I said, and Vo jumped to his feet with his fist in the air.

"I knew it!" he exclaimed, then turned to the other two. "Pay up."

I'd guessed they had a bet going, of course. If it was one of them keeping secrets, I would've been in on the bet too.

"So you don't want to know the rest?" I asked, and Vo quickly resumed his seat.

"Sorry, sorry. Keep going," he said, holding his palms up.

"His name is Elian. He's a forest spirit," I said, and Quill's eyes went wide.

"The one who lives in the park?" he asked, and I nodded.

"Wow. How did you figure it out? I don't think I've ever seen him around the place. I just assumed he has a secret hideout somewhere," Quill said, his blue eyes alight with curiosity.

"Or he lives in the trees," Vo said before I could continue, and Quill turned to him.

"He can do that?"

"Yeah. All forest spirits can sort of possess their land. Travel through the trees, use their magic to make the plants grow bigger and healthier...stuff like that," Vo explained and I nodded along in agreement.

"That's so fucking cool," Quill said, and I knew right then he was going to be Elian's biggest fan. I'd need to warn Elian about him. Not everyone could handle Quill's exuberance.

"Can I ask why you waited so long to tell us? Not that you had to share, of course," Vo said, and I adjusted my glasses as I tried to think of the best way to phrase this.

"Elian is a very private person. In fact, I myself met him face-to-face for the first time just a few days ago. I was worried that if I told you guys, you might want to get to know him, and he wasn't ready for that," I said, and Quill pursed his lips in thought.

"Fair enough," he declared after a minute, and I felt myself relax. The last thing I wanted to do was hurt my friends' feelings.

"Does that mean he's ready to meet us now?" Vo asked as he leaned back into the couch.

"I'll have to ask him," I said, and Vo nodded in understanding.

"Fair enough. And I promise I won't try to go see him until you tell me it's okay," Quill said, making me smile. Maybe I should've given my friends a little more credit. "But it's a good thing you waited until now to tell me, because if I had known about Elian when you were moping, I would've given him a visit for sure." Then again, maybe not.

"I guess I do know you guys well, then," I said, and Quill stuck his tongue out at me.

"So, the cat's finally out of the bag," Memphis said, and I exhaled deeply. Not having a secret anymore felt good.

"Yes, it is. I'm really happy for you, Alden. You deserve to have a happily ever after," Quill said with a wide, genuine smile.

"You sound like your writer mate," I teased, and he shrugged.

"His words are as beautiful as he is. Of course I'm gonna quote him sometimes."

"You're such a sap," Memphis teased, and Quill rolled his eyes.

"You're one to talk. You turn to goo when you're around Orion."

"I think it's safe to say you're all very much in love with your mates," I cut in before the conversation could devolve into another meaningless argument. Being the dad of the group was tough work, but someone had to do it.

"All right, guys. I need to take off. Trick will have to get to work soon, so I have another chance to win the Best Dad trophy," Vo said as he stood up, and I chuckled at his enthusiasm. I'd known Vo would be a great dad since the day he held baby Neel in his arms for the first time, and he'd proven me right over the past few months.

"Go on then. We'll see you later," I said, and he gave us a salute before heading toward the door.

"I should get going too. We're going to have a movie night, and I need to make sure they pick the right movie," Quill said, and I chuckled. Quill could be such a snob sometimes. Luckily for him, his mates seemed to love that about him.

Once Quill had left, it was just Memphis and me in the living room. Orion was still with the boys—the Mistvale kids were having a playdate, which I'd considered myself lucky to be spared from having to participate in—and as far as I knew, it was Memphis's day off from the pub.

"Wanna play a game?" Memphis asked, motioning toward the console, and I grinned.

"Sure, why not?" Nothing sounded better at that moment than defeating Memphis.

Elian

The tree I used to store my phone alerted me that it'd made a sound, and I made my way through the park before shifting into my human form once I was in my garden. It was almost midnight, and I wondered who was texting me at this hour. Only two people had my number, and I could guess which one of them it was.

Plucking the phone out of its spot, I unlocked it and smiled when I found a message from Alden waiting for me.

Alden: I told the other two about you today.

Me: You did? How did it go?

Alden: About as I'd expected. They asked me if they could meet you, and I told them I'd have to ask you about it.

I chewed on my lip as I thought about that. I liked Orion, and I adored Alden. But he had a lot of friends, and I didn't know if I could handle that many people.

Me: I don't know if I'm ready to meet them all.

Alden: That's okay. They promised they wouldn't push, and I believe them. There is something else we could do, though.

Me: Yeah? What is it?

Alden: I have a group text with the guys and their mates. I could add you to it, and you could get to know everyone before you meet them in real life.

I smiled at Alden's message, enamored by his thoughtfulness. How had I gotten so lucky as to end up with someone like him?

Me: That sounds fun. It was how I became friends with Orion.

Alden: Exactly. Once you feel comfortable talking to them, then we can see about meeting up.

Me: Thank you.

Alden: What for?

Me: Accommodating me. Understanding me.

Alden: It's my pleasure, I assure you.

Alden: I'll add you to the text tomorrow, okay? If I do it now, the others will annoy me about trying to 'sneak you in.'

Me: Haha, I understand. Are you heading to bed now?

Alden: Yeah, just wanted to talk to you before I slept :)

Me: I'm glad you texted. Is it weird that I missed you even though we spent the day together?

Alden: If it is, I'm just as weird.

I laughed at his message, then wished him a good night before finally putting my phone away. Taking a deep breath, I shifted into my true form before lying on my log. Brushing my roots against the trees around me, I convinced them to straighten up a little so I could look at the stars.

The past few days had been blissful to say the least. Alden and I had spent the day together every single day, and we'd both been in our human forms. We'd talked about inane things, mostly, but it had still felt wonderful to be able to answer Alden's questions and ask my own.

Alden had brought cupcakes and tea the other day, and we'd eaten them together. Alden had offered me bites from his, and then stolen some of mine. It had felt wonderful.

I couldn't remember the last time I'd felt this...happy. Hell, I couldn't even remember the last time I'd *felt* this much. Life as a dryad was pretty monotonous most of the time, and after centuries of living the same day over and over again, this change of pace felt magnificent.

Closing my eyes, I could almost imagine Alden beside me. Not in his human form, no, but in his majestic unicorn form. His beautiful, colorful hair gleaming in the moonlight, his pure white coat glowing softly, his violet eyes that somehow looked otherworldly even with the horn sticking out of his forehead.

Alden was an ethereal being, the last of his kind, and I was the lucky bastard who got to be with him for the rest of my life. It felt like a blessing, a reward for some good I must've done in a previous life, and not just because of what Alden was.

He might have been a unicorn, but all my favorite things about Alden were much simpler than that. I loved how patient he was, how confident in his own skin. I adored how much he enjoyed eating the fruits I brought him, and how obviously he loved his family. Alden was warm and kind and sweet, and I liked all of those things about him.

Fate had changed my life the day she led Alden to this park, and I would forever be grateful for that. I was sure that if we hadn't crossed paths, I would've still been the same old Elian, hiding away in my trees and wanting nothing to do with the outside world.

I'd changed a lot over the past few months, and I was proud of myself for it. After losing so much of my land to the humans, I'd been determined to never form any kind of connections again. Alden had managed to break my resolve, and I was glad he had. No matter how much I'd tried to deny it, my life before him had been utterly lonely, and I'd grown tired of it.

The visitors to the park had offered me some entertainment, but more often than not, they'd just made me wish I had someone like them in my life. Now, it seemed, I did.

Letting out a sigh, I turned on my side, smiling when a cool breeze washed over me. Would it rain, perhaps? My trees always loved it when it rained, and therefore so did I. It was why I'd been so happy when I sensed the presence of a storm dragon in Mistvale a few years ago, and even happier when I'd felt him claim the town as his own. He had no hold over *my* land, but since it was a part of the town, his magic gave my park a second layer of protection too, which I wasn't going to complain about.

After meeting Alden, I knew the storm dragon's name was Raiden, and he was the leader of the Mistvale clan. While the Mistvale clan was the largest interspecies clan I'd heard of, now that the supe population of Mistvale had grown, there were other supernatural groups in the town too. The newer residents had so far stayed away from my park, and I hadn't yet decided if I was going to allow them in. I trusted the Mistvale clan, but I had no idea what kind of people the newer residents were. I knew the dragon would've vetted them with his magic before permitting them inside the town, but I still wasn't going to allow just anyone to come waltzing into my park.

As sleep finally drew close, my thoughts drifted back to Alden. I was looking forward to spending another day with him, and also getting to know the people he was closest to, even if it was just through texting.

THIRTEEN

Alden

I strolled through the streets, the bag of cupcakes and tea firmly clutched in one hand. It was just past nine, and while I usually visited Elian after ten, I hadn't wanted to wait today. Now that we were finally hanging out together, with both of us in our human forms, I longed to spend all my time with Elian. I just hoped he didn't get sick of me.

The moment I stepped through the entrance of the park, a wave of comfort washed over me, relaxing limbs I hadn't even been aware of being stressed. I made my way to our clearing, biting back the urge to whistle.

It wasn't just my growing relationship with Elian that had me in such a good mood, though it was a big part of it.

I was also happy because on my trip to the bakery today, I'd sensed a lot more supes than I usually did. The supe population in Mistvale had been growing faster and faster over the past year, and I had a feeling the day wasn't far when Mistvale would be a completely supernatural town.

Raiden had texted me the other day, asking if I'd be willing to meet up to discuss the whole thing, and I'd said yes, though we hadn't set a date yet. I did not want to be in Raiden's shoes right then. He must have been working his powers to the max to make sure no unsavory supes made their way in.

Maybe I could offer him a helping hand. My instincts might be able to help root out the bad eggs.

"Good morning, Alden," Elian greeted me as soon as I stepped through the trees, and I smiled widely as I met his bright green gaze.

"Morning, Elian. Did you sleep well?"

"I did! What about you?" he asked, and then his eyes lit up as they slid to the paper bag in my hand.

"I slept like a baby, thank you. I brought breakfast," I said, and he nodded quickly before moving to the log.

"Tell me the truth. Do you just want me for the cupcakes?" I demanded, trying to infuse my voice with all the mock outrage I could muster up.

The question finally made him look at me, and he rolled his eyes. "Yeah. You caught me," he said in a voice devoid of any inflection, and I cracked up.

Placing the bag of goodies on the log, I shook my head as I smiled at him. I loved the fact that Elian had finally started loosening up around me. I was also starting to realize he had a snarky streak that only showed when he felt comfortable. It was now my goal in life to make him sass me as much as possible.

As we munched on the cupcakes and drank our tea, I told Elian about my upcoming meeting with Raiden and the growing supe population of Mistvale. Elian told me he hadn't decided yet if he was going to allow the newcomers into his park, and I assured him that Raiden would never allow anyone with bad intentions to live in Mistvale.

"That's true. Do you think one day there would be no more humans left in the town? At least none that don't know about the supernatural world?" Elian asked, and I hummed thoughtfully.

"It's possible. More and more humans have been moving out recently, or getting bought out by supes at exorbitant prices. The word seems to have spread in supe communities that Mistvale is a safe place for supes, and they've been moving here in droves. I think it's very likely that within the next decade, Mistvale will become a completely supernatural town," I said, and Elian shook his head.

"It feels strange to imagine something like that, but I think it could be wonderful too," Elian mused, and I nodded in agreement.

A town where supes were free to be themselves without the fear of being spotted or revealing their existence? It sounded like a dream, but one I'd love to see turned into reality.

Once we were done eating, I packed up all the trash before turning to Elian.

"Do you want to meet the others now? On text, of course," I asked, and Elian's eyes widened before he nodded quickly.

"Let me get my phone," he said, and then between one moment and the next, he'd disappeared. It took me a second to realize he was using his land to travel, and I wondered how exactly that worked. Could he carry things through the place the same way, or was it limited to only allowing him passage?

My question was answered when Elian stepped through the trees a few minutes later. Guess it was limited.

"Okay, I'm ready," he said as he settled beside me, and I smiled at his enthusiasm.

Unlocking my phone, I scrolled through my text threads to find the right one. We had a whole bunch of text groups, one with just the four of us, one that also included our mates, one with the whole clan, and one with the whole clan and some of the older kids. All the groups were also extremely active, which meant I always had at least a few messages waiting on my phone, no matter the time.

Opening the thread with my best friends and their mates, I quickly added Elian's number and then sent a quick introduction post.

Me: Everyone, I'd like you to say hi to my mate, Elian.

There was a few seconds of silence before the first message pinged both our phones.

Quill: Oh my God, finally! Elian, it's so good to meet you! I'm Quill.

Elian: It's nice to meet you, Quill. I've heard a lot about you.

Memphis: All bad things, I hope. :P Hey, Elian. Welcome to the family. I'm Memphis.

Vo: And I'm Vo. It's so nice to meet you!

Elian: Hello, Memphis and Vo.

Orion: We meet again, Elian. Hope you're ready for these three. They're a riot.

Elian: I hope so too :) I would like to get to know Alden's family better.

Quill: Aww, you're so sweet. I think we're going to be great friends, Elian.

Joy: Oh wow, we have a new member! Elian, hey! I'm Joy, Quill's better third.

Trick: I really need to remember to put you guys on silent.
Trick: Wait.
Trick: Elian, hello! Sorry about that. I'm not fully awake yet. Had a night shift.

Elian: It's so good to meet all of you.

"You okay?" I asked, worried all of them piling on was getting too overwhelming for Elian.

"I'm fine," he assured me, then gave me a smile that helped a lot more to assuage my worry. "They're nice."

"They can be when they try really hard," I joked, and Elian smiled as his phone pinged again.

Maybe I should've waited until this evening before introducing them.

Elian

Alden's family was the friendliest bunch of people I'd ever encountered. Not that I'd talked to many people in my lifetime, but I had observed quite a lot of supes and humans.

My phone pinged again, and I smiled as I unlocked it.

Tate: What did I miss?

Tate: Oh, hello newcomer! I'm Tate, Quill and Joy's mate.

Joy: He's the peanut butter to my jelly.

Quill: And what am I?

Tate: You're the bread, obviously.

Joy: Obviously.

I blinked, a little confused and a little amused by the conversation I was witnessing.

"They do that a lot," Alden said, and I realized he was staring at his screen too. "Our conversations rarely stay on topic for more than a few minutes. They're a bunch of goldfish, all of them."

I chuckled at the disgruntled look on Alden's face, but I could tell he wasn't actually annoyed. He adored his friends immensely, even if they did sometimes drive him crazy.

Since it looked like they'd finished greeting me, I put my phone away and smiled up at Alden. "Thank you for introducing me to them."

Alden shook his head as he reached out and took my hand in his. Carefully, I shifted closer to him, and his smile brightened. "It was my pleasure, Elian. I've been wanting to for a while now. I'm glad I finally got the chance."

I smiled at the look of happiness on his face, and my eyes slid to his mouth. What would it feel like to press my lips against his? Did Alden even enjoy kissing? We'd talked about our mutual disinterest in sex, but I had no idea if Alden included kissing in that.

I decided the best thing to do was to ask. Knowing Alden, he'd answer the question honestly and without making me feel like it'd been the wrong thing to say.

"Alden," I said, my voice hushed as if I was about to tell him a secret.

"Yeah?"

"What is your opinion on kissing?" I asked, and Alden raised a brow at me.

"Kissing?"

Nodding slowly, I let my eyes flick to his lips once so he'd know exactly what I was talking about. "Yes. Do you enjoy it?"

Alden blinked, and I watched as his Adam's apple bobbed with a swallow. "I-I do."

"Then, may I kiss you?" I asked, and Alden's grin widened as he nodded.

Shifting even closer to him, I pressed my leg against his as Alden leaned toward me. Placing my palm on his cheek, I sifted my fingers through his silky hair as I slowly brushed my lips against his before pulling back to check his reaction.

Lavender eyes met mine, and Alden leaned forward to press his lips against mine, his hand curling around my hip as he held me close.

Warmth spread in my chest as Alden's lips danced, and I kissed him back as I slid my fingers into his hair, combing through the silky blond hair.

Something hard dug into my cheek as Alden changed the angle, and I pulled back in confusion. "Oh," I said when I realized it'd been his glasses, and reached for them. "Can I remove these?"

"Yeah, sorry," he agreed with a wince, and I smiled as I pulled them off.

"Why do you wear these anyway? It's not like you need them, right?" I asked, and Alden gave a smile I'd call sheepish.

"I don't, no. I just like the way I look in them," he said with a shrug, and I smiled.

Tilting my head, I roamed my eyes over him and hummed. Then I slid his glasses back on and nodded to myself.

"Oh yes, I see it. You look like a scholar with them on," I said, and Alden chuckled.

"I do? And what do I look like without them?" he asked, and I pursed my lips thoughtfully.

"A rogue pirate," I decided after a moment, and Alden's brows shot up.

"A pirate, really?" he asked, voice ringing with disbelief, and I shrugged.

"A leather headband, some vines from around here tangled in your hair, and you'd fit the part perfectly," I joked, and Alden rolled his eyes.

"You, on the other hand..." Alden murmured thoughtfully, and I scrunched my nose. Uh-oh. Was he going to cast me as well?

"Oh, I know. You'd be a great Pan," Alden declared, and I tilted my head to the side thoughtfully. I was pretty sure I'd heard the name before, but I couldn't remember the person at all.

Alden seemed to realize that from whatever look I was sporting because he pulled his phone out and started typing.

"Here," he said, showing me the screen. On it was a man who looked like a satyr. "He's the Greek God of the wild. A being all the little animals flock to."

While there weren't many similarities between us, I found the name acceptable enough. After all, I couldn't deny my connection with Mother Nature.

"So you're a pirate, and I'm Pan," I concluded, and Alden chuckled.

"Yep, sounds about right," he said with a grin, and I shook my head.

Now that I was finally getting used to spending time with Alden, I couldn't remember what I'd been so worried about. All my anxiety seemed pointless from the other side, but there was no point in mulling over it now.

"I think I'd like to kiss you again," Alden said after a moment, and I smiled up at him.

"I'm not stopping you," I assured him, and he smiled before leaning closer and pressing his lips to mine.

FOURTEEN

Alden

A few days later, I was on my way to the park after a late morning. It was the weekend, so I'd spent the morning with Neel and Pax. I'd texted Elian about it, and he'd told me to take my time. I'd finally managed to get away at noon after getting teased by Memphis *and* Orion. Clearly, Orion was starting to get affected by Memphis's bad influence.

I was almost at the park when a familiar feeling pulled me up short. My magic stirred inside me, alerting me that something was wrong. While my magic was strong, it was also based on and expressed through instincts, which meant it wasn't always clear.

Right then, I got the feeling something was happening or had happened that would affect Elian, but he himself wasn't in any danger yet.

I focused on the feelings I was getting in the hopes that I could sense exactly what was wrong, but I couldn't get a clear picture. All I could tell was that the solution wasn't at the park, and that the problem was related to Elian's land.

There was one person who might have an idea of what was going on, but before I asked him, I needed to let Elian know I might be even later.

Me: Hey, Pan. Something came up, so it'll take me a bit to get there.

Elian: No worries. See you soon. <3

Smiling, I switched to my thread with Raiden and sent a text.

Me: Hey, are you free? There's something I need to talk to you about.

Raiden: I was just about to text you. I need to speak to you too. Meet me at the park in 10?

Me: The park? Why there?

Raiden: Because this concerns your mate too, as I'm sure you already sensed.

I wasn't even going to ask how Raiden knew Elian was my mate. Hell, he'd probably known before I did.

Me: Okay.

I debated between telling Elian in text or face-to-face, and decided I could get there before Raiden to warn him in case he didn't want to be around physically.

I made it to the park with five minutes to spare, and found Elian sitting in our clearing, surrounded by a bunch of critters. Huh, maybe I should've named him Snow White.

"You're here!" Elian said when he spotted me, and I smiled as I approached him. Something on my face must've clued him in because his brows drew close.

"What's wrong?"

"My magic told me something was happening that would affect your land, so I texted Raiden to see if he'd heard any-thing, and he said to meet him here in a few minutes. He said whatever he has to say concerns you too."

Elian blinked at me a few times, and I realized I'd blurted a whole lot of words all at once.

"So Raiden is coming here?" Elian asked after a long pause, and I nodded quickly.

"Yeah, he is. If you want, I can talk to him alone. It's completely up to you."

"I'll stay," Elian said after a moment, and I smiled in relief. While I would've been okay, I wanted Elian by my side. Being away from him every night was all I—and our bond—could handle. Maybe after we'd dealt with whatever this issue was, I could talk to Elian about staying the night.

"He's here," Elian said as he shot to his feet, and I followed after him as he left the clearing and headed toward the entrance.

"Hey, Raiden!" I called when I spotted him, and his stormy gray eyes met mine as he smiled.

"Hey, Alden," he said, and then turned his focus on Elian, holding his hand out as he introduced himself. "Hello, I'm Raiden Hawthorne."

"Elian. Nice to meet you," Elian said as he shook his outstretched hand, and I felt a burst of pride fill my insides. Elian had progressed so much in the short time I'd known him. It wouldn't be long before he was ready to step out of his land.

"Please, come this way," Elian said, and Raiden glanced at me before we both followed Elian to another small clearing with a couple of fallen logs arranged across from each other. Had this spot always been here? I'd have to ask Elian later.

"So, do you know what's going on?" I asked, cutting to the chase. I would've focused more on the pleasantries if whatever was going on didn't concern Elian. Then again, it wasn't like Raiden was a guest. We'd become good friends since I moved to Mistvale, even if we didn't hang out all that often.

"I believe so. I heard from a contact at the city office that someone is trying to buy this land to build an apartment complex," Raiden said, shocking me into silence.

"That's...can they do that?" Elian demanded, and the fear in his voice made me shift closer on the log we were sharing and take his hand in mine.

"The land is owned by the government, and while they wouldn't usually sell it, if the buyer is a supe, which I suspect they are, we have to assume they have some kind of power they can use to convince whoever needs convincing," Raiden said, and I shook my head.

"We can't let that happen," I said, glancing over at Elian before turning to Raiden. "This land is Elian's home. They're connected."

"I know. They haven't made a purchase yet, so we still have time. I thought we could talk to them and explain the situation. I have a feeling if they knew the land was claimed, they'd understand," Raiden said, and I frowned. I didn't know if that would be enough to dissuade someone, but then again, dryads were held in high regard by most supes. At one point, humans and supes alike had prayed to dryads and naiads for better crops, fresh water, fish, and many other things. While supes no longer prayed to dryads, they still considered them to be a step above most supernatural beings.

"It's worth a try," I said, glancing at Elian when he cleared his throat.

"Would it help if I came too?"

Elian

While I'd thought of stepping outside my land before, I'd never actually made a plan to do it, especially anytime soon. But if it helped to protect my land, I would.

I didn't want to keep my land because I liked owning it, but because it was an important part of Mistvale. All the trees and little animals in this park depended on me to keep them safe and healthy, and I had no doubts that whoever wanted this land had no plans of letting my flora live. They probably wanted to destroy the park and build something in its place. Something full of concrete and devoid of greenery. I couldn't allow that to happen.

"It won't hurt if you did, but you don't have to. You know that, right?" Alden asked, and I smiled at him. It was sweet how worried he was, but this was my problem to deal with. I appreciated his help, of course, and Raiden's too. I wasn't going to stop him from doing whatever he wanted to do to help, but this wasn't on him. I was going to talk to whoever this person was, and I was going to inform them the Silent Creek Park was not for sale.

"How about this? I'll find out who the buyer is and set up a meeting with them. I'll let you both know the time and place, and you can decide if you both want to go or not. Would you like me to be there?" Raiden asked, and I thought about it for a minute before nodding. Raiden was a dragon, and the one who watched over this town. I didn't think any supe would want to be on his bad side, and that could work in our favor.

"Don't worry, okay? Everything will be fine. We won't let anyone take your land from you," Raiden said, and Alden squeezed my hand.

"Yeah. You have the whole clan at your back. You have absolutely nothing to worry about," Alden said, and there wasn't a shred of doubt in his voice.

Smiling up at him, I leaned into his side, letting myself relax now that we had a plan.

Raiden pulled his phone out of his pocket and checked something before looking up at us. "I need to get going. I'll text you the details as soon as I get them."

"Sounds good. Thank you for helping," I said, and Raiden smiled.

"You're part of the family now, Elian. Of course I'd help. Let me know if you need anything. Have a good day, both of you."

Alden and I walked Raiden to the park's entrance, and then made our way to our clearing.

"Would you like to spend some time in our true forms? You don't have to talk if you don't want to," Alden asked, and I smiled. How did he know just the right thing to suggest?

"Yes, please," I said, and between one moment and the next, Alden was a beautiful, regal-looking unicorn.

Stepping close to him, I ran my palm over his warm, silky coat, and ran the fingers of my other hand through his colorful hair.

"You're beautiful," I murmured, leaning forward to press a soft kiss on the soft plane of Alden's muzzle.

Moving back, I shifted into my true form, exhaling deeply as my skin changed color and hardened, as roots spilled from my arms.

Alden made a soft, neighing sound and shuffled closer, pressing the side of his head against my hip. Smiling, I wrapped an arm over his neck, resting my forehead against his side. He felt so warm and steady, like someone I could lean on, a pillar of support who'd always be there for me.

After we'd stood there in our pseudo-hug for a few minutes, Alden started moving.

I pulled back to see what he'd do, and he trotted around the clearing a few times before picking a spot and lying down. Apparently, Alden wanted to take a nap, and the idea sounded pretty good to me too.

Walking over to him, I sat down beside him, prompting him to make a soft, welcoming sound. He nudged me with his nose and it took me a moment to realize he was telling me to move closer.

Alden lay with his legs folded under him, and I pressed myself against his side, leaning my whole body against him. Like before, he supported my weight completely, and I ran my fingers over his soft fur as I soaked in his warmth.

Closing my eyes, I lay my head against him, enjoying the steady rise and fall as he breathed. The movement slowly lulled me toward sleep, and I allowed myself to float, trusting Alden to keep me tethered.

I wasn't sure how long I slept, but when I woke up, it was dark, and I felt much more relaxed than I had before.

Sitting upright, I focused on my land to make sure nothing was amiss, and once that was done, I turned my attention to the beautiful unicorn who was still lost in sleep.

Sometime during our nap, Alden had shifted so he lay on his side, and his head rested in the grass, a few stalks moving rhythmically as he exhaled on them. I wished I had my phone close by so I could take a picture, but since I didn't, I memorized the moment as best I could.

Closing my eyes, I could see Alden clearly. Relaxed and asleep, with his limbs curled up and his rainbow hair splayed out on the grass, he looked like this was exactly where he belonged, like he was another integral part of the park.

Maybe someday he would actually stay here, with me and all the little critters that lived on my land. If that happened, I would want for nothing more in this life. Having Alden with me every minute of every day would be a wish come true, and I could very easily imagine a life with him.

Opening my eyes, I found deep violet eyes gazing at me, and I ducked my head, hoping he hadn't realized I'd been daydreaming about us.

Alden gave a soft neigh, and I returned my gaze to him. He made another sound, and for some reason, it made me feel like he was assuring me that he felt the same way, that he was prone to daydreaming too.

FIFTEEN

Alden

"I texted them to let them know I won't be coming home tonight," I said, and Elian nodded, the light flush on his cheeks darkening a little.

"Are you sure you're okay with me staying?" I asked, and he nodded quickly.

"Of course! I'm happy to have you here. I promise," he said, and I believed him. We were both a little excited and a little nervous about this new step, and it showed.

My stomach growled, and I realized I'd need to eat dinner that included more than fresh fruits if I wanted to feel full.

"Hey, what do you say about trying some human food for dinner?" I asked, and Elian pursed his lips thoughtfully before nodding.

"What were you thinking?"

"Well, Trick's a chef, and he works at an Indian restaurant that has a vegan menu. I thought maybe we could order something from there? I can go pick it up in a bit," I offered, and Elian nodded quickly.

"That sounds good. I don't know much about Indian cuisine, so can you order for me, please?"

"Of course," I assured him with a smile before pulling my phone out. The restaurant didn't actually offer takeaway or delivery, but being friends with the head chef helped in times like this.

Me: Hey, Trick. I need dinner for two from the vegan menu. Any recs?

Trick: Oh, I made a great veggie kofta today, if I do say so myself. The veg pulav will go well with it, along with some roti.

Me: All of that sounds delicious. How soon can I pick it up?

Trick: Give me 15.

Me: You got it.

"It'll be ready in fifteen minutes," I said, and Elian nodded before scanning the clearing with his eyes. He seemed a little fidgety, but I guessed that was due to the prospect of me staying the night.

"I was thinking...it would be better to sleep in the garden. You'll be more comfortable there," Elian said, and I glanced over at him. His eyes were resolutely focused on the trees, and I smiled to myself as I answered.

"You think so? I don't mind sleeping here," I said, patting the log I was sitting on. If it got too uncomfortable in my human form, I could just shift and rest on the ground. It'd been a while since I'd slept in my true form, but the nap I'd taken earlier had been blissfully peaceful. I credited a large part of that to Elian and the park, because I'd never felt as safe anywhere else. Hiding what I truly was had been a second-nature to me until I met Vo and the others, but even after that, I'd never felt completely safe shifting into my true form. Until now.

"No, the garden is big enough for us both," Elian said firmly, and I dipped my head in acceptance. I hadn't seen Elian's garden yet, but if he was ready to share it with me, I wasn't going to decline the invitation.

Fifteen minutes later, my phone pinged with a text from Trick telling me our food was ready, and I rose to my feet. Elian did the same and took my hand in his before leading the way toward the exit.

"I'll be right back, okay? Thirty minutes, tops," I said, and Elian squeezed my hand.

"Okay, I'll be waiting. Be careful," he added, and I winked at him before taking my leave. It was just a little past nine, and the streets were filled with an evening crowd. The crowd was mainly made up of supes, with a human here and there, and it felt good to be surrounded by other magically inclined people. Even if I'd never come across anyone who was exactly like me, supes still felt a lot closer to 'my people' than humans.

Then again, my past experiences with supes weren't all that much better. The humans, the few I'd revealed myself to, usually hadn't known what to make of me. The supes on the other hand—at least the older ones—had known a little more about my powers, and about what I could do for them.

I shook my head to clear my thoughts when I reached Pait Pooja and walked inside, approaching one of the servers to let them know Trick had an order for me. Practically all the employees at the restaurant now knew that Trick's family was made up of a bunch of foodies, and we ordered from them often enough that no one had a problem with us using our connection with Trick to get takeaway every once in a while.

Once I had our food, I paid for it, thanked the server, and made my way back to the park, increasing my pace a little so the meal wouldn't go cold. When I reached the park, I made my way to our clearing and stopped short when I found it empty.

"Elian?" I called as I set the bag of food on the wooden log, and when I didn't get a reply, I debated if I should go looking for him.

Before I could make up my mind, Elian stepped through the trees with his hair in disarray and looking like he'd run a marathon.

"Everything okay?" I asked, taking a step in his direction. He flashed me a bright smile before walking closer, and took a deep breath.

"Everything's fine. That smells lovely."

"It does, doesn't it? My stomach hasn't stopped growling since I started walking back," I said, and Elian chuckled.

It was only once I'd started unpacking that I realized we didn't have dishes. If I'd remembered earlier, I could've asked Trick for some, or bought some paper plates from a convenience store.

"It's all right. We can make this work," Elian said with a confidence I was lacking, and I blew out a breath as I started opening the boxes.

In the end, we ended up sharing the kofta straight from the box and holding the rotis in our hands. Luckily, they *had* included spoons with the pulav, though we did share it from the same box, which should've felt romantic but wasn't. Maybe that only worked when you were eating something sweet like ice cream or cake.

"That was wonderful," Elian said once we were done, then patted his stomach for emphasis. I smiled at the utter cuteness of him, and he blushed when he found my eyes on him.

"It really was," I agreed wholeheartedly.

Elian

When Alden had left to get dinner for us, I'd taken a few minutes to move things around in my garden to ready it for him. I'd never, ever had another person in my garden before, and I would never allow anyone else to step foot in that space. Anyone except Alden. Alden was my mate, and therefore, what was mine was his too. I wanted to share my private area with him, and I hoped he'd like it as much as I did.

After we'd finished eating, Alden packed up all the trash, and then we spent a while chatting. Now that things were calming down, worries about the supe who wanted to buy my land started cropping up in my mind again, but I did my best to push them back and focus on Alden's words.

Alden yawned for the third time as he told a story, and I decided it was time to sleep. Nerves filled me, but for a completely different reason this time.

"How about we head to the garden? I think you're ready to sleep," I said, and Alden opened his mouth, a protest clear on his face, but yawned before he could get a word out. I raised a brow at him, and he huffed before standing up and holding his hand out to me.

"Let's go, then," he said, and I smiled as I took his hand and let him pull me up. He didn't let go of my hand as we started walking, and I led the way to the very edge of the park where it met the creek. The entrance to my garden was hidden in plain sight in a narrow opening between two trees, but no one had ever accidentally wandered inside, so it worked perfectly for me. I'd debated over closing it up for good since I could just travel through the trees, but now I was glad I hadn't.

"Oh, I never noticed this," Alden said as we stepped through, and I smiled at the wonder in his voice.

I stopped once we were inside, giving Alden a chance to take everything in.

The garden was my safe space, and I'd modeled it to be a warm and cozy space. The trees here had thick trunks, big leaves and many branches, with flowering climbers clinging to their trunks and surrounding the area with color and fragrance.

The trees also understood my needs perfectly. Like right then, the sky was clear, so the branches were raised up, giving me a clear view of the night sky. But if it were to start raining, they'd lower and stop the water from raining down on me. Not that I had any problem getting wet, but it was hard to sleep with water sprinkling on you.

The ground was covered in a thick layer of grass that was perfectly dewy in the morning and cushioned my feet the rest of the day. On one side, there was a small path that led down to my own little section of the creek. On the other side was a path that led a little deeper into the park where my hidden orchard was.

To complete the cozy atmosphere, I had wildflower bushes edging the clearing, with blooms of all colors brightening up the space. The bees the flowers attracted filled the air with a soft buzz, and the faint fragrance the flowers gave always made the area smell just a little minty.

Of course, Alden probably couldn't see most of it in the dark, but he'd wake up to this beautiful sight tomorrow, and that was just as good.

"What do you think?" I asked when Alden had been quiet for a few minutes, and he glanced over at me, his eyes wide with awe.

"It's beautiful. I used to think the park was magical, but this...it's on a whole different level," Alden murmured, then whipped around to face me. Reaching out, he took my other hand in his and stepped closer, his lavender gaze burrowing into mine. "You are wonderful, Elian. The things you create with your magic..." He trailed off with a shake of his head, his gaze roaming all over the garden before returning to me. "I know you're still worried, but I promise—the clan and I won't let anyone take your land from you, okay? The Silent Creek Park belongs to you."

My eyes started burning in a way they never had before, and I blinked repeatedly to get them to behave. Alden had guessed correctly. I was concerned. But hearing his assurance eased the building worry in my mind. I trusted Alden, and for once in my life, I wasn't alone. Every time before when my land had been threatened, I'd protected it alone. It was why I'd lost a part of it every time. But this time, things would be different. This time, I wouldn't have to fight alone.

"Thank you," I said in a low, thick voice, and Alden smiled as he stepped closer. When he leaned forward, I pressed my lips to his without hesitation.

We kissed as the crickets chittered around us, as the leaves moved in the light breeze, and I felt more at ease than I had in a while. Kissing Alden felt comforting and warm, like drinking a warm drink in the middle of winter. It was some time before we pulled away, and I led Alden to the sleeping area I'd set up for us.

"I set us up on the ground in case you wanted to sleep in your true form," I explained, and Alden nodded as he slipped out of his shoes at the edge of the makeshift mattress. I let go of his hand so he could move around better, and I settled on his knees on the mattress. He ran his palm over the grassy top before digging his fingers in, a look of surprise on his face.

"It's so soft," he murmured, and I smiled as I joined him from the other side. I'd made it large enough to accommodate his unicorn form and me, so if we wanted, we could sleep on opposite sides without ever touching. Not that I wanted that, but he might. He hadn't had a problem sleeping side by side in our other forms, but things were different in this form, weren't they?

"The garden helped," I said by way of explanation. The trees had offered me a whole host of almost-dead leaves that were still healthy enough to be soft, and the creepers and climbers had offered parts of themselves to layer over the leaves. The bugs and ants had also given me their word that they wouldn't come anywhere near us for the duration of the night.

"Well, let them know I'm very grateful," Alden said as he lay down before patting the space beside him.

Smiling, I lay down as well, and turned so I was facing him. There was still space between us, and while I was tempted to slide over and wrap my arms around Alden, I held back.

Alden smiled at me as he removed his glasses and put them away, and then gave a big yawn. Chuckling, I said, "Sleep, Alden."

"Yeah, okay. Night, Elian."

"Goodnight, Alden," I murmured as he closed his eyes, his long, pale lashes brushing against his skin. I watched him as my thoughts circled round and round, his assurances from earlier muting in the face of my anxiety.

My focus returned to Alden when he stirred, and he reached out an arm to pat the space beside him. "Come here," he mumbled, then peeked one eye open. "I can almost hear you worrying. Come here, Pan."

Carefully, I shifted toward him, and as soon as I was close enough, Alden wrapped an arm around me and tugged me closer until our chests were pressed together. I moved so my head was tucked under his chin, and Alden made a happy sound. "There. That's better. Now, sleep, Elian. Everything will feel better tomorrow."

Surprisingly, or maybe not so surprisingly, I fell asleep minutes later.

SIXTEEN

Alden

It'd been a long, long time since I'd last woken up with a dick poking me in the ass. I'd never been interested in sex, but there had been a period where I'd done with anyone who was willing in an attempt to figure out what was wrong with me. It had taken me way too long to conclude that nothing was wrong with me, and that not wanting sex wasn't the end of the world.

Still, waking up with my mate's dick poking me made me wish I was. Elian had said he wasn't interested, but what if he'd said that for my sake? Then again, I couldn't put too much stock in biological reactions. After all, I got morning wood too, and I knew what I wanted. Or didn't want, as it were.

How I'd ended up as the little spoon was still a mystery to me, but I decided to enjoy it for a few more moments. Being wrapped up in Elian's arms was comforting, and being surrounded by his garden was even more so.

Last night, I'd observed the place in complete darkness, and I'd still loved what I'd seen. But now that the sun was rising, I felt like I was in a fairy tale. Hell, this place might just be better than the stuff of fairytales. Maybe something closer to a garden from Faerie, the land of the fae. Then again, dryads were distant cousins of the fae, so that wasn't far from the truth.

Elian stirred behind me, and I held still, not wanting him to realize I'd been awake and still enjoying being held by him.

I hadn't really thought much of cuddling before. Not until a few years ago.

When Neel was four, he had a two-year phase where he wanted to cuddle with everyone. Whoever was on the couch got roped into snuggling with Neel and watching a movie, and whenever he had a nightmare, he would sneak into one of our beds and wrap himself around us like a koala bear. It'd taken me a while to realize I looked forward to my turns, and I'd been very down when Neel had grown out of that phase.

"Good morning," I said after a minute, and I felt Elian startle behind me. His arm around me tightened and then loosened as he pulled away, and I turned around to face him as he spoke.

"Good morning, Alden. Did you sleep well?" he asked, and I hummed.

"Oh yeah. I think I might just sleep here every night. I haven't slept that deeply in a while," I said as I stretched my arms above my head. Then I realized what I'd said, and my eyes went wide. Elian didn't seem to be too affected by my declaration, which made me wonder if he'd heard it at all.

"I wouldn't mind that," he said, telling me that he had. "I slept well too. I don't usually sleep this long."

"Up before the sun, hmm?"

"Yes. I like watching the sunrise. And it takes a while to check in with all the plants, and if I wake early, I'm done by the time you arrive," he explained, and I blinked in surprise.

"Wait. Does that mean you wake up early because of me?" I asked, and he shook his head.

"No, I've always done that. It's just one of the perks," he explained.

"You need to check in with them now, don't you?" I asked, and Elian nodded as he sat up. I followed suit, then glanced down at my wrinkled clothes.

"How about you do that while I go home, shower, and change? I'll pick up some breakfast on my way back," I offered, and Elian nodded quickly.

"That sounds good. Have you heard from Raiden yet?" he asked, and I realized his worries had already returned.

I picked up my glasses and my phone from the ground, slid them on, and unlocked the phone. There were a few texts in the group chats that I ignored for now, but nothing else.

"He hasn't texted yet. I'll let you know as soon as he does," I said, and Elian nodded. Rising to my feet, I pulled him up after me and dusted myself off before taking a look around.

I'd missed a lot of the smaller details last night. Like how the giant log on the far side was covered in a thick layer of moss, making it look like it'd grown out of the ground as-is. The trees around us had similarly thick trunks, but instead of moss, they were covered in various climbing plants, blooming with flowers in various colors. The whole place was an explosion of colors, bright, cheerful, and safe. I could hear water too, and quite close. This must have been the side that edged up against the creek. Was there a path here that led right to it? Maybe we could take a walk later.

My phone beeped, and I checked the screen to find a 'battery low' sign flashing back at me.

"I should get going. Need to charge my phone as well," I said, and Elian nodded.

Leaning forward, I pressed my lips to his in a quick peck before taking a step back. "I'll be back soon."

"I'll be waiting," Elian said with a soft smile, and I winked at him before turning around and heading toward the exit. It took me a moment to find the corner where the garden's exit hid, but once I was out, the rest of the way was familiar.

When I got home, I had five seconds of joy thinking no one was home. I'd barely tiptoed across the hallway and reached the base of the stairs when Memphis spoke and scared the shit out of me, not that I'd tell him that.

"Oooh, look who's still dressed in clothes from last night," he said in a teasing voice, and I turned around to face him.

"Hey, Memphis. Where's everyone?"

"Orion went to drop off the kids. It was my turn, but I needed to be here when you got back, so I convinced Orion to go," he explained, and I rolled my eyes. I should've known I'd get the third degree. He wasn't going to let me go until he got every last detail of my time with Elian, especially since I'd stayed the night. Luckily for me, I had a lot of experience dealing with Memphis.

"Someone's trying to buy Elian's land," I said, and the smirk on Memphis's face disappeared instantly.

"What? Seriously? Who the fuck would do that?" he demanded, all teasing thrown aside, just like I'd expected.

"Raiden says it's a supe. He's going to set up a meeting so we can convince them not to," I said, turning around and sitting down on the stairs. I didn't think I'd be able to get away without a proper conversation now.

"And if they don't agree?" Memphis asked, and I shrugged.

"I don't know what I'll do, but I won't let them take Elian's land from him," I said, and Memphis patted my knee.

"Good. We won't let anyone steal your mate's home," he said in a voice brimming with confidence, and I smiled at him.

"I told Elian as much, but he's still worried," I said, and he nodded understandingly.

"I bet he's dealt with shit like this before. Dryads used to have acres of land once. I bet his land used to be much bigger," Memphis said, and I had to agree.

We'd never talked about it before, but I was sure Elian had once controlled all the land that was now called Mistvale. He'd already lost so much of his land already. I wasn't going to let him lose another foot of it.

"Let us know if you need any help, okay?" Memphis said, and I nodded.

"I'm gonna go grab a shower," I said, and he nodded quickly and stood up, offering me a hand.

Pulling myself up, I tugged him into a hug. Memphis returned the hug, his arms tight and reassuring around me. "Stop worrying. Everything will be okay."

"Yeah," I murmured as I stepped back. "I know."

Hurrying up the stairs, I walked down the hall to my room. After plugging my phone into the charger, I headed into the bathroom.

I contemplated taking a bath, but I wanted to get back to Elian quickly, so I decided on a shower instead. Afterward, I'd pick up some stuff from the bakery before heading back to the park. Maybe some strawberry cupcakes. Elian loved those.

Elian

Alden returned before I was done checking on all the trees, and I apologized to the rest as I hurried through them faster than I usually would.

Once I was done, I found Alden waiting in our clearing, a familiar paper bag sitting on the log beside him.

"Sorry I made you wait," I said as I approached him, and he waved me off.

Taking a seat beside him, I waited while he dug through the bag, pulling out two Styrofoam cups of tea.

I took the one he handed me, removed the lid, and took a sip, humming at the warm, delicious liquid as it slid down my throat.

Alden smiled as he sipped his own tea, and we gazed into each other's eyes like two lovesick fools.

By the time I swallowed the last of it, my cheeks were flushed, and I quickly looked away under the pretense of putting the cup away.

Alden pulled out my favorite cupcakes from the bag, and I mentally cheered before taking one from the box.

"How do humans come up with food this delicious?" I mumbled through a bite, and Alden chuckled.

"I have no idea, but I hope they never stop trying to cook up new things," he said, and I nodded in complete agreement.

Once we'd finished our breakfast, I packed everything up and stored it in a corner for Alden to take away later.

"Hey, I meant to ask. Your garden shares a side with the creek, right? Do you ever go that way?"

"Hmm? Oh, yes, I have a path that leads to the bank. It's a strip of land where people rarely come, so I go there sometimes at night to look at the water. Would you like to see it?" I asked, and Alden nodded.

"Yes, please. I've been to the creek before, of course, but I like seeing it from different places. Plus, it's a good place to take a walk."

"That's true. Come on, then," I said, holding out my hand. Alden smiled as he took it, and we headed toward the creek.

"You don't shift into your true form often, do you?" I asked as we made our way down the path from my garden. It was a question that had been in the back of my mind for a while, but I'd never gotten around to asking it before.

"No, I don't," he said, shooting me a smile before turning his attention to our surroundings. "My unicorn form makes me feel... vulnerable, even though I'm physically stronger in that form. In the past, I haven't had the best experiences when people came across me, and now I don't feel comfortable shifting unless I'm in a place I feel safe. I can't do it at home because I'd be too big, so I shifted very rarely before. The others would come with me to the woods when I needed to shift, so it wasn't so bad."

"You feel safe shifting at the park, right?" I asked after a moment, and Alden stopped walking. He turned to face me, a smile on his lips, and placed his free hand on my cheek.

"I've never felt as safe anywhere else as I do at the park. Knowing that you won't allow a stranger to get anywhere near us is all I need to be able to shift," he said, and I smiled. I was glad he felt safe at the park, and with me. I had no idea what kind of experiences he'd been talking about, but I could tell they hadn't been pretty. I never wanted Alden to go through anything like that ever again.

It may have taken a long time for us to cross paths, but now that we had, I was determined to make sure Alden never, ever felt unsafe again.

"Come on. It's only a couple of minutes away," I said, and Alden dropped his hand as I started tugging him toward the creek.

"Wow, it's beautiful," Alden said in a soft voice when we reached the bank of the creek, and dropped his hold on my hand to turn in a circle to admire the area.

The spot I frequented was overflowing with flora, with all kinds of wildflowers blooming in huge bunches around us. There wasn't a strict place to sit, but we made some space at the very edge of the land and sat down with our feet in the water, our pant legs pulled up to our shins.

"This is nice," I said, and Alden smiled over at me.

"Yes, it is. Thank you for sharing it with me," he said, and I returned his smile, reaching out to take his hand again.

"It's my pleasure. I like sharing things with you," I admitted.

"Me too. Whether it's cupcakes and tea or stories about my family, everything feels better when I share them with you," he said, and then ducked his head, a hint of red flaming up his cheeks. "That sounded dorky."

"I have no idea what dorky means, but I adored everything you said, and I feel the same," I said seriously, and Alden glanced over at me from beneath his long lashes.

"You're a very sweet man, Elian," he said, and it was my turn to glance away. Sometimes, I was still surprised by how far I'd come. It hadn't been that long ago when I'd been hiding away from Alden, and now here we were.

"And you're a kind one," I said once I'd found my voice, and Alden smiled as he pulled me into his side.

Resting my head against his shoulder, I watched the water move. Everything about the moment calmed me down and put all my worries on hold. What would happen if this moment never ended?

SEVENTEEN

Alden

We returned to the park just around noon, and decided to sit in our clearing instead of the garden. Somehow, the garden felt too intimate during the day, and since we'd need to get some lunch in a while—unless Elian convinced me to try a fruits-only diet, which wasn't happening anytime soon—we figured the park would be better.

Elian had been telling me about his past, about the time when he'd controlled all the land of Mistvale and even beyond, back when all of it had been a forest.

Hearing the way the humans had taken away his land, I wished our paths had crossed before. We'd both spent a long time on our own, alone and afraid with no one to rely on. How different would our lives be if we'd met a few centuries ago?

"What about you? You said you only met the others a while ago. Were you alone before then?" Elian asked, and for the second time today, my thoughts returned to my old life.

"I was, yes. I found it hard to trust people. It took me a while to trust Vo, Memphis, and Quill too, but they taught me how to. Before I met them, I would drift from place to place, and do my best to hide what I was," I explained, and Elian nodded thoughtfully.

"That sounds so lonely. I'm glad you found the others. Was it truly that bad if someone found out you were a unicorn?" he asked, brows furrowed, and I sighed.

"Not always. Sometimes, the people I came across were just in awe of me, or wanted me to use my magic to help them in some way. But every once in a while, I'd come across someone who wanted my power all for themselves. Or someone who wanted to use me to boost their own magic," I said, then smirked. "Apparently, unicorns are pure beings of light, and our blood can be used to power great spells."

"That's awful," Elian murmured, then shifted closer on the log so he was pressed against my side. Smiling, I wrapped my arm around his middle and enjoyed the way he leaned into me. "Is that how your horn broke?" he asked after a moment, and then quickly added, "You don't have to tell me if you don't want to talk about it. I'm just being nosy."

"It's okay," I said with a small laugh. "It's been a long time since it happened."

I wrapped my free hand around the tip of my horn that always hung on a cord around my neck, sensing the power buzzing in it. My power.

"Centuries ago, I was traveling through Europe when my magic alerted me that something was wrong. It urged me to turn around, to leave, but there was some spot I'd been wanting to see, and I thought I'd be able to deal with whatever problem cropped up," I started narrating, and my mind returned to that cold morning, to the chill in the air, and the way the wind had blown through my mane.

"I'd been in my true form because I was traveling through a forest. I'd wrongly assumed it was too cut off for people to be anywhere close. At that time, people still believed in dragons and unicorns, and just like my magic had warned me, a few such people found me. I'd have been okay if they were all human, but one of them had been a skilled warlock, and they trapped me. They had a master, a ruler who wanted to use my power to expand his empire."

"That's terrible. I can't imagine how scared you must've been," Elian murmured, and I hummed softly.

"Yeah. At first, I kept thinking that I'd figure a way out, that even if they had captured me, they would never dare to hurt me. But the king had heard that a unicorn's power was in his horn, and he thought that if he cut off a part of it, he could have some. He told me he was going to be benevolent and only take a part of it," I scoffed, remembering the moment as clearly as if it'd happened just yesterday.

"So he broke your horn to steal your powers? But you still have it, so something must've gone wrong."

"Yeah, it did. After, he realized neither he nor the warlock had any way of accessing or using my powers. The horn had magic, but only I had the ability to use it," I explained, and Elian chuckled.

"Sorry. I know I shouldn't laugh, but knowing that they didn't get what they wanted makes me happy," Elian said, and I couldn't resist pressing a kiss against his temple.

"It's okay. I know I did. Right at his face. He was angry, but there was nothing he could do. I had to get out of there, so I acted like the lack of my horn had weakened me. It wasn't long before they let their guard down at the wrong time, and I made my escape."

"I'm glad you got away, but I'm sorry they hurt you," Elian said, and I waved him off.

"It's okay. I don't feel bad about it anymore. I can still use my magic to its full extent as long as the horn is touching my skin. Usually, I slip it over my shirt so I don't always have to see everyone's aura. I wouldn't be able to do that if they hadn't broken it."

"I suppose that's a silver lining," Elian said, his eyes latching onto my curled fist before moving up to meet my eyes. "Can I touch it?"

Nodding, I pulled my hand away from the piece of my horn and waited. Somehow, it felt more intimate than any other way Elian had or could've touched me. My horn was the source of my magic, and it was precious to me. The only other people I'd allowed to touch it were Neel and Pax. Lena also grabbed it whenever she wanted to, but she didn't exactly need or ask for my permission.

Elian

Though I'd asked to touch the piece of Alden's horn, I felt a little nervous as I reached out to brush my fingers against it. It was such an integral part of who Alden was, and I felt like I was about to brush his soul.

The moment I touched the horn, Alden lit up with a light bright enough to make me squint. I sucked in a breath as I jerked my hand away, and the light disappeared instantly.

"What is it? Are you okay?" Alden asked, and I blinked rapidly to clear my vision.

"I—uh, you were glowing. When I touched your horn, your whole body lit up. Didn't you feel it?" I asked, glancing up into his worried gaze, and he shook his head.

"I didn't, no. Can you give it another try?" he asked, and I nodded slowly.

Taking a deep breath, I reached out and touched the smooth horn again. Like before, Alden lit up, and I squinted as I stared at him, but didn't pull away.

"What do you see?" Alden asked, and I tried to find words to describe what I was seeing.

"Your skin has a shimmer, of sorts. It's mostly white, but it gets tinges of different colors every now and then," I explained, and Alden gasped softly as the light around him flared orange for a second.

Letting go of the horn, I sat back and watched him. "You know what I was seeing, don't you?" I asked, and he nodded. The look of awe on his face made my heart beat faster, but I ignored it for the moment and waited for him to tell me what it was.

"You were seeing my aura," he said, and I stared at him, confused.

"Your aura?"

Alden nodded, then reached up to hold his horn again. "It's one of my powers. When this is touching my skin, I can read people's auras. It's why I always keep it over my shirt unless I need to use it. You...you accessed my powers, Elian."

I blinked at him, completely stupefied. "You said that wasn't possible."

"I guess there are exceptions. Like if the person trying to gain access is my mate," he said, and I shook my head in wonder. I could access his unicorn magic? Wow.

"That's..." I trailed off, unable to come up with an adjective good enough for the situation.

"I know. It's cool. I didn't think I'd ever get to share my experiences with anyone else. Not like this," Alden said, and I smiled at the enthusiasm in his voice.

"Well, I'm glad I get to share it with you then. You'll have to teach me how to read auras though. I could see the colors, but I had no idea what any of them meant," I said, and he smiled.

"Of course. It'd be my pleasure."

The buzz of a phone interrupted whatever he was going to say next, and he pulled his phone out of his pants pocket.

"It's Raiden," he said as he flicked open the text chain, and my heart jumped. I'd almost forgotten about that, about the person who was trying to buy my land. How could I have let something so important slip my mind?

"He says he got in contact with the guy who wants to buy the land. He's asking if it would be okay to invite him to meet here." Alden glanced at me as he spoke, and I wondered what emotion my face was showing.

On one hand, I didn't want that man anywhere near, but on the other hand, maybe seeing it would help him see the fact that this land was exactly as it should be, and that he had no right to destroy it.

"They can come here," I said finally, deciding to deal with the discomfort if it meant keeping my park safe. I'd have Alden with me too, and I knew he'd keep me from getting too overwhelmed, or even take over if I did get too out of it.

"Are you sure?" Alden asked, telling me he could see through me. I nodded as I ran my palm over the log we were sitting on.

"He should see the place he wants to destroy," I said simply, and Alden watched me for a moment before nodding and returning his attention to his phone.

Raiden and Alden exchanged a few texts before he put his phone away, and I waited for him to speak, ignoring the way my heart was beating like a drum.

"They'll be here in an hour," Alden said, and I nodded quickly. Alden moved closer and wrapped his arm around my back, pulling me into his body.

"Hey, everything will be okay. You've got Raiden on your side, remember? No supe would dare go against a dragon, a unicorn, and a dryad, trust me," he said, and when he put it that way, it was hard to doubt him.

Alden and his friends were so...warm and good that I sometimes forgot they were also powerful supes in their own right. I'd only talked to Raiden once, but I had observed him a few times before that, and the way he acted camouflaged his immense powers so well that no one could suspect just how strong he was. It was what made him truly dangerous. I was glad to have him on my side.

"Thank you," I said in a low voice as I wrapped an arm around Alden's middle and clung to him. I didn't know what I would do without his support, and I didn't want to imagine it.

"You don't need to thank me for anything, Elian. I'm glad I'm here with you," Alden replied, and I felt him press a kiss against the top of my head.

Turning my head, I pressed my lips against his chest, only a thin layer of cotton separating us. I felt brave enough to face the man who wanted to take my land from me because I knew he wouldn't succeed. For once, I wasn't alone in my fight, and that was why I would win.

EIGHTEEN

Alden

The man who'd scared Elian for the past two days wasn't very imposing. For one, he was a vampire. While I knew two very impressive, very kind vampires, my opinion of their kind as a general wasn't very high.

Most vampires were indulgent, greedy beings, and while I didn't know this man well enough to judge him, his aura told me he enjoyed the finer things in life. I'd only been around him for two minutes though, so I decided to gather a little more data before making any kind of decision about him and his motives.

"Calix Taylor," the vampire said, holding his hand out, and I took it and gave one firm shake before pulling my hand away. Calix Taylor was a good-looking man—as most vampires were. He had perfectly styled brown hair, sharp blue eyes, and was dressed for a business meeting, which in a sense this was. I doubted he'd ever had a work meeting in a park though.

"Alden," I introduced myself, then took Elian's hand in mine. "He's Elian. This is his land."

"Mr. Hawthorne explained to me that this park belongs to you, Elian. But you don't have legal ownership of it, right?"

Calix asked, and Elian's grip on my hand tightened considerably. I wondered if I should field the question, but Elian answered before I could.

"I've raised this land since before this town existed, Mr. Taylor. I don't need a piece of paper to prove it," Elian said, and I blinked in surprise. I'd never heard Elian sound that assertive.

Calix raised his hands up in surrender before taking in the park. We'd seated him in the same clearing Elian had used when Raiden came over earlier, and I was surprised when I saw splashes of green in his aura. Wonder and awe. He was actually impressed by what he saw.

"Can I ask why you want to buy?" Elian asked, and I glanced from him to Calix. Elian already knew why, of course, but I supposed he wanted to hear straight from the vampire's mouth.

"Of course," Calix said, leaning forward as he started speaking. His aura lit up with a dark pink I associated with passion, and my brows shot up. This man kept surprising me at every turn, it seemed. That would teach me for judging him after two minutes of meeting him.

"Well, Mistvale has turned into a safe haven for supes in recent years, and a large number of supes have moved here since. There are even more supes who would like to move here but can't because of the lack of living space. Mistvale used to be, and still somewhat is, a tourist town. There just aren't enough homes here. I want to build an apartment complex for supes," Calix said, and there wasn't a shred of dishonesty in his words. He truly meant every word he'd said, which meant he wasn't a bad person at all.

"That is actually a wonderful idea," Raiden said, echoing my thoughts. "We can't build it here, of course, but I can't deny more living space would be a good thing."

"I honestly didn't know this land was claimed by a dryad when I asked about it at the town office," Calix said, and I had no choice but to believe him since he was telling the truth.

"It's okay. We all make mistakes. I'm sorry I can't help, but I've already lost a lot of my land, and I can't afford to lose any more," Elian said, and I squeezed his hand comfortingly.

"I understand," Calix said, smiling faintly. "I'll figure something out."

"*We* will figure something out," Raiden corrected him, and Calix glanced at him with a puzzled look on his face. Uh-oh. It looked like another member was going to be dragged into the Mistvale clan.

"We will?" Calix asked, confusion clear in his voice, and Raiden gave him a big smile.

"Yes! I'm sure the Mistvale clan will love to help with this, and together I'm sure we can come up with a viable solution. Come on. We can talk about this on the way back," Raiden said, and stood up.

"Elian, Alden, thank you for talking to me. And I apologize for any discomfort I caused you," Calix said, and Elian smiled at him as I did the same.

"It's all right. Just let us know if you need any help with the apartment complex," I said, and he stared at me for a moment before shaking his head. His aura was a mess of confusion, and I felt for the poor guy. When I'd first arrived in Mistvale, I'd been dumbfounded by how easily everyone had accepted me and the others. The Mistvale clan was one of a kind, and Calix was about to learn just how helpful they could be when they put their mind to it.

We walked Raiden and Calix to the entrance, and then waited until they'd driven off before returning to our clearing.

Once there, I sank to the ground and lay on my back, spreading my arms above my head as I let my body relax.

"What are you doing?" Elian asked with laughter in his voice, and I squinted at him as he hovered over me.

"Just enjoying the land we so valiantly protected," I joked, and Elian chuckled loudly before lying down beside me. I turned on my side so I could see him, and winced when the hard dirt dug into my hip.

"One second," Elian murmured. I watched as he placed his palm flat on the ground and closed his eyes. Slowly, grass started pushing up from the dirt, and within minutes, we were lying on a thick layer that was soft and very cushiony.

"You take such good care of me," I said, a barely there teasing lilt to my voice.

"As do you," Elian said as he shifted closer to me and wrapped an arm around my waist.

"You were so good with Calix. So assertive and firm," I praised, and Elian smiled in satisfaction.

"I could only do that because you were there with me," he said, and I scoffed.

"I think you're secretly a badass, and you just don't want anyone to know," I said, and then mentally rolled my eyes at myself. What was I even saying? I was being all dorky again.

"If I was, I'd tell you," Elian said, and I smiled as I gazed at him. Leaning forward, I rested my forehead against his, soaking in his touch. I could do this all day and never get tired of holding him.

Elian

Moving my head just a little, I pressed my lips to Alden's. He hummed under my touch as he kissed me back, and I let myself sink into the sensation of warmth that kissing Alden always filled me with.

Alden felt warm and comfortable and mine, and I held on to him as I continued kissing him. I felt magic stir in the land below us, but I ignored it in favor of kissing Alden some more.

When I finally pulled away so we could catch our breaths, Alden gasped softly. At first, I thought he was just having trouble breathing, but then I saw what he must've spotted first.

All around us, from the grass I'd grown earlier, flowers bloomed in a multitude of colors. Pink, orange, red, and lavender blooms filled the area around us in a rough circle. Alden reached out and brushed his fingers over the petals of a red flower, a wide smile on his face.

"You did this, didn't you?" he asked, and I shook my head.

"I think *we* did this," I corrected him, and his eyes widened as he turned his attention back to the flowers. I'd sensed the magic stirring, yes, but I'd also sensed it wasn't all mine. Maybe my skin had accidentally brushed against Alden's horn, or maybe it was our kiss, but something had helped our powers combine and create this.

"It's so beautiful," Alden murmured, and I smiled.

"It is," I agreed as I reached out to touch a lavender bloom. Slowly, I convinced the plant to let me have the flower, and it fell into my palm.

Smiling, I gathered a few of them in different colors before turning to Alden.

"Could you sit up for a moment?"

Alden gave me a curious look before doing as I'd asked, and I went on my knees so I could reach him properly.

Moving around until I was behind him, I slowly wove the flowers I'd collected into his hair. He had beautiful platinum hair, and it was frizzy enough that I could make the flowers stay without using pins of any kind.

"Are you putting flowers in my hair?" Alden asked, his voice a mix of curiosity and exasperation, and I hummed in answer.

"They look good, I promise," I assured him, and he grumbled something nonsensical that I chose to ignore.

When I was done, I told him to stay still and hurried back to my garden to fetch my phone. Alden had taught me how to take pictures the other day, and also how to set them so I'd see it every time I unlocked the phone.

I was glad to see Alden sitting exactly as I'd left him, and I walked over until I was in front of him before going on my knees again.

"Oh my God, are you really going to take a picture of me like this?" Alden asked, and his cheeks went bright pink when I nodded.

"You look beautiful," I assured him, and he sighed, telling me without words that he wouldn't stop me. "Now, smile please?"

I took a whole bunch of photos, much to Alden's annoyance. But then he convinced me that we needed a few pictures of both of us, and he insisted on sticking some flowers in my hair as well.

Then we decided we should take some pictures in our true forms, just for fun. I was worried about them getting into the wrong hands, but Alden assured me that even if some human saw it, they'd think it was made up and fake.

We had to set the phone on the log, and start a timer on the camera to take a proper picture, but we did it, all with the flowers still woven into Alden's mane.

By the end of our impromptu photoshoot, we had around fifty pictures in total. Some of them were blurry, but most of them were utter perfection.

"That was actually pretty fun," Alden said as we sat on the ground looking through the pictures, back in our human forms. We'd taken them all on my phone, and then Alden had sent them to his phone.

"I want to meet your friends," I said, the words popping up out of nowhere.

Alden turned to look at me in surprise, and I shrugged. I'd surprised myself a little too, and I didn't quite know what to say next.

"Really? You feel ready?" Alden asked.

"I do. I mean, I've met Orion, Raiden, and even a stranger. I've been talking to your friends in chat for a while now. I'm sure I'll have fun spending some time with them," I said, and I realized I meant it. While I might feel a little nervous at first, I was nowhere as anxious as I'd been at the beginning.

"How about I invite just Vo, Memphis, and Quill first? If that goes well, we can invite their mates too next time," Alden suggested, and I agreed quickly because three people sounded a lot better than seven for a first meeting.

"Okay, would you like to do this today or tomorrow?" Alden asked, and his stomach growled before I could answer.

Chuckling, I shook my head. "We can talk about it later. First, let's get you something to eat. How about some fresh apples and strawberries?"

"Sounds delicious," Alden said with a smile, and I got to my feet before holding out a hand for him.

Once he was on his feet, I led him to the garden. Before, we'd only spent time in the central area of my garden, but now I led him to my small orchard.

"Oh wow, I didn't even realize this place existed. You're very good at keeping these spots hidden," Alden said, and I grinned at the praise.

"You can pick whatever looks good to you. They're all fresh," I said, and Alden hummed as he carefully examined the trees and the fruits they bore.

"What happens to the leftovers?" he asked, and I walked closer to him, picking a strawberry and popping it into my mouth.

"There are none. These won't go bad if I don't allow them to, so we can take our time," I explained, and Alden's brows shot up.

"You're pretty powerful, aren't you, Pan?" he mused, and I shook my head at the silly nickname.

"Maybe I am, *pirate*. You aren't so bad yourself," I pointed out, and he smiled a smirky little smile that made me want to kiss him senseless. So I did.

NINETEEN

Alden

The next day, I left for the park with the assurance from Memphis that they'd drop by around Quill's lunch break. Since Memphis worked nights at the pub and Vo was taking a break from his security job—a break I was sure was going to become permanent—it was only Quill's occupation at the auto repair shop that they needed to worry about.

Personally, I'd never gotten into the whole job thing. I'd collected some precious possessions over the years that I could now sell for a ridiculous amount of money if I needed to, but on a daily basis, I made it work with the returns I got from the investments Raiden had convinced me to make. The man was a wizard with money, and I didn't think anyone in the clan would ever be lacking for funds thanks to him.

When I arrived at the park, Elian was waiting for me just beyond the entrance.

"Oh, hello! Didn't expect to see you there," I said as I stepped closer to him, and he smiled before popping up on his toes and pressing a chaste kiss on my lips.

"I was just excited to see you," he said, and I smiled as I took his hand in mine and started walking toward our clearing.

"Is that so? Any particular reason why?" I asked, and he shrugged.

"Not really. I missed you last night, I guess," he said, and butterflies fluttered in my belly at the admission. I'd missed him last night too, and I'd almost walked here twice.

"I missed you too. I wish I'd stayed the night. It took me hours to fall asleep," I admitted, and Elian glanced over at me.

"I barely got any sleep either. Maybe you should stay the night from now on."

"I just might," I said as we reached the clearing, and sat down on the log. A few strawberries were waiting for me, and I handed Elian the bag of tea and cookies in exchange.

We sipped our tea and snacked on the cookies as I told Elian about Memphis and Co.'s plans to visit around noon.

"I'm looking forward to meeting them. I feel like I know them already," Elian said with a smile, and I returned it as excitement brewed in my gut.

Some very important people to me were going to meet for the first time today, and I really wanted them to get along. Then again, Memphis, Vo, and Quill had never met anyone they couldn't befriend if they wanted to, so I was sure everything would be okay.

By the time they finally showed up, I was probably even more excited than Elian was. Having all the people I loved—or almost all, since Neel and Pax wouldn't be there—in the same place felt better than anything.

Wait, love?

Memphis's voice pulled me out of my thoughts, and I shook my head, deciding I'd think about that particular four letter word later.

Elian hid behind me as first Memphis, then Vo and Quill stepped through the entrance.

"We're sorry about this," Vo said, and before I could ask what he meant, Orion, Trick, Joy, and Tate spilled through one after the other, mirroring sheepish smiles on all of their faces.

"Why did I ever think you'd listen?" I demanded as I scrubbed my palm over my face. I should've known better than to think they would've left their mates out of it.

"Hello." Elian's voice made me remove my hand, and I realized he was peeking out from behind me and waving at the others. Fuck, he could be so damn cute sometimes.

"Hey, Elian. It's so good to meet you. Sorry about the crowd," Memphis said as he took a few steps closer to us, and Elian stepped out from behind me with a smile on his face.

"It's okay. Come on, we can sit and chat," Elian said, and Memphis shot me a wink as we all followed Elian to what I was now going to call the guest clearing.

"Wow, I keep forgetting just how beautiful this place is," Joy said as we reached the clearing, and everyone claimed spots on the logs scattered around the space.

"You're welcome to drop by whenever you like. Even if I'm not present like this," Elian said as he waved at himself, "I'll still be around."

"We will. We were just staying away the past few months because of this one," Quill said as he pointed at me, and I rolled my eyes at him.

"I never told you to stay away from the park. I just told you not to follow me," I reminded him, and he stuck his tongue out at me.

"Potayto, potahto," he mumbled, and I shook my head.

"It's nice to finally meet you, Elian. I know it can feel a little overwhelming to go from living alone to being surrounded by people, but you'll get used to it," Tate said, and I smiled. I still remembered the first time we'd met. Back then, Tate hadn't had his sight yet, and I assumed everything had been even more taxing for him because of that. He'd still powered through, and now he was just as active in clan-related things as anyone.

"That's good to here. I'm glad I met you guys, but I also think that texting with all of you first helped immensely," Elian said, and I squeezed his hand gently.

"I'm glad. We know we can be a little too much sometimes," Vo said as he scratched the back of his neck, and Memphis chuckled.

"By which he means Quill and I," he said, and I rolled my eyes. He wasn't wrong, after all.

"Oh, has Alden told you the story of the first time we met?" Vo asked, and my eyes widened.

"Oh no, you don't!" I said, scrambling to cover his mouth before he could say another word.

"Oh, come on! Let him tell it! It's not like he's the only one who knows," Quill protested with a laugh, and I reluctantly let him go.

"You'll pay for that," I assured Vo as I resumed my seat beside Elian, and he shook his head at me, completely unafraid. He might be a strong-as-fuck gargoyle with skin that could turn to stone, but I had a few tricks up my sleeve. I'd known him for centuries, after all. I knew exactly what made him tick.

Elian

Within hours, I felt like I'd known Alden's friends forever. I'd never truly had friends before I met Alden, and now I had so many of them. It was a wonderful feeling.

Quill, Memphis, and Vo were having fun telling me stories about Alden, like why his mane was rainbow-colored. Apparently, a few years ago, a much younger Neel had wanted Alden to look like the unicorns on TV, so Alden had changed his mane with his magic and fallen in love with the colors himself.

While they told me stories about him, Alden promised them retribution for it. I could see how close the four were, and it made me happy, especially after Alden had told me how lonely he'd been before he met them. I was intimately familiar with loneliness of that kind, and while I'd never found *my* Quill, Memphis, and Vo, I'd found Alden, and through him, all these amazing men.

"Oh, I almost forgot!" I said as I remembered something. "I'll be right back."

Leaving the others behind, I hurried over to my garden, grabbed one of the baskets I'd made when I was bored, and started picking some of my best fruits for the group. I'd meant to do this before, but I'd gotten distracted.

Once I had a good collection of fruits, I headed back to the others. Alden smiled when he spotted me, and I returned it as I placed the basket on a small log in the center.

"These are from my garden," I said, returning to my seat beside Alden.

"Ooh, fresh fruits? Don't mind if I do," Trick said as he left his seat to pick a few of the berries. Settling beside his mate, he offered one of the strawberries to Vo, who grinned as he bit into the fruit without taking it off Trick's hand.

"Holy shit, this is delicious!" Quill exclaimed, and I glanced over at him to find him munching on an apple.

"It really is. I guess this explains why Alden made such a face that day when I made him eat a store-bought apple," Memphis said with a chuckle, and Alden shrugged beside me. "The man's been spoiled with all these freshly grown fruits."

"You're welcome to take some home whenever you like," I offered, and I meant it too. My orchard was never lacking, and now that I had people I could share them with, I wanted to.

"I'll take you up on that. I can already imagine all the things I could bake with these," Trick mused, and I smiled. Thanks to Alden, I'd fallen in love with baked sweets of all kind, and the thought of fruits from my garden being used filled me with joy.

"I'd love to try whatever you create," I said, and Trick grinned.

"Of course. You'll be the first to get a sample," he assured me, despite Vo's loud protest. Apparently, mates should get 'first dibs,' whatever that meant.

By the time the group was ready to leave—Quill had texted his boss and asked for the rest of the day off. Since he almost never asked for leave, his boss had allowed it—it was around four in the evening.

"We'd stay longer, but we need to go pick up the kids," Orion said apologetically, and I waved him off.

Honestly, as much as I'd enjoyed spending time with all of them, I wasn't used to it, and I was starting to feel the need to retreat. To me, it felt like the perfect time to stop.

"Yeah. We left Lena with them too, and while I trust Noel to look after her, it's still a little unsettling to be away from her for so long when neither of us are with her," Trick said, and I smiled. They were all such good people, and I was glad I'd gotten the chance to know them.

"I'd love to have you back again," I said, and I meant it. As tired as I felt right then, I also felt a sense of accomplishment. And happiness.

"Maybe we could bring the kids next time? Neel's been asking about you," Orion suggested, and I felt Alden's eyes on me.

I glanced over at him to find him watching me with hopeful eyes. I knew he had a soft spot for his friends' kids, and while I didn't have a concrete opinion, I was sure I'd be able to handle these men's children.

"That sounds fun," I said, and Orion grinned.

"We'll set something up," Memphis promised, and I nodded. Maybe in a few days, though. I needed some time to recuperate.

Alden and I walked the others to the entrance, and all the while, the talking never stopped.

"Will we see you at home tonight?" Memphis asked as we reached the entrance, and Alden stole a glance at me before shaking his head.

"I don't think so," he told Memphis, and I bit back a smile. While I would like to be alone, Alden was the exception to that rule. Being around him was never stressful, at least not now that I knew him well. I'd love it if he stayed the night again.

"Okay, then. See you tomorrow. It was great to meet you, Elian," Memphis said, and the others echoed his sentiment.

Returning the gesture, I leaned into Alden and watched as they all got in their vehicles and drove away. Once they'd disappeared from view, I turned to Alden and wrapped my arms around him, tucking my face into his neck and allowing myself to relax.

Alden wrapped his arms around me tightly and supported my weight, like he could sense how tired I was.

"That wore you out, huh?" he murmured into my hair, and I gave a minuscule nod. "How about we go take a nap in the garden? That should help," he suggested, and I sighed gustily before pulling back.

"Sounds good," I said, mustering up a smile for him.

"If you want, you can take a shortcut. I'll catch up," he said, and it took my tired brain a minute to figure out what he meant.

"You don't mind?"

"Of course not. Go, I'll be right there," he assured me with a smile, and I nodded before melting into the closest tree. Traveling through my land was faster and also less taxing since the trees gave me power just as much as I gave them nourishment.

Just that short trip had me feeling better when I arrived in the garden, and when Alden showed up a few minutes later, he quickly dragged me to bed and wrapped himself around me.

With my head resting on his shoulder and my arms curled up between us, I took one of the best naps I'd ever had.

TWENTY

Alden

I'd almost forgotten about the meeting Raiden had asked me to attend until I woke up to a text from him asking if I was free this morning.

My plans for today had included lazing about with Elian and helping him relax after yesterday's adventures, but I didn't want to skip out on this meeting, not if it concerned all of us.

I also hadn't heard anything about what happened with Calix Taylor. Had he found a different land to build on? Had Raiden helped him?

"Is everything okay?" Elian's voice pulled me out of my thoughts, and I turned to watch him as he sat up, rubbing the sleep out of his eyes. God, he was so beautiful. His hair shone green in the sunlight that had snuck through the trees, and his bright green eyes seemed to sparkle when he finally removed his hands and looked at me.

"Uh, yeah. Everything's all good. I just got a text from Raiden. Remember that meeting he asked me to attend about the growing supe population? He wants to do that today," I explained, and Elian nodded slowly.

Reaching out, I ran my fingers through his hair, smoothing out some of the sleepy tangles. Once that was done, I trailed my fingers over his cheek, admiring the soft skin. He didn't have any stubble. I was pretty sure he didn't have any other body hair at all, other than his brows and hair. I didn't know if it was a part of him being a dryad or a personal choice—I was sure his magic allowed him to choose whether or not he wanted hair at any particular spot on his body, just like mine did—but either way, I loved how smooth it made his skin feel.

"When do you have to go?" Elian asked in a hushed voice, and I glanced up at him.

"Uh, he wants to meet at the packland at eleven," I said, though most of my focus was still on my fingers, watching them trail over his dark skin.

"That's on the other side of town, right? So you'll need to leave at least thirty minutes early," he said, and I hummed in answer.

"How can you look so beautiful right after waking up?" I asked, and Elian glanced away, his cheeks heating up under my touch. After a moment, he returned his gaze to me, pressing his cheek a little harder into my touch.

"You say that, and yet *you* don't have a single hair out of place," he said, reaching out to tug a strand of my hair. "How do you explain that?"

"Um, I brushed it before you woke up?" I suggested with a grin, and he rolled his eyes.

"Or one of the perks of being a unicorn is always looking perfect," he mused and I scoffed.

"I'm hardly perfect," I said, and Elian smiled.

"Maybe not. None of us are. But you are the most beautiful man I've ever seen," he said, and it was my turn to blush. My reaction made his smile widen, and he leaned forward to press his lips to mine.

After we'd made out for a while, Elian sent me home to shower and dress in fresh clothes so I didn't look like a hobo—my words, not his—for my meeting with Raiden.

Memphis found me the moment I stepped through the doorway, and I told him about the meeting to get out of being hassled by him.

After a quick shower, I got dressed, brushed my hair—I hadn't, in fact, done that before—and grabbed my phone from where I'd put it to charge before heading downstairs.

"You have time for a quick cuppa, right?" Memphis asked, and I checked the time on my phone before nodding.

Memphis made us both tea, and I settled on a barstool to sip mine.

"Yesterday was fun," Memphis said, and I glanced up at him. He'd chosen to stand on the other side of the counter, and it was the only time I had to look up to meet his eyes.

"It was. Elian really enjoyed having all of you over. Even if you did ignore his request," I said, and he gave me a sheepish grin.

"Sorry. I guess we're just too weak against our mates' wills. You'll see," he said in a confident tone, and I didn't doubt him. Finding your mate changed something fundamental in you.

For Memphis, it was that he finally felt completely comfortable in his skin, in his decisions, in the way he lived his life.

For Quill, it was that his search had ended. He finally had a family of his own, and parents in Joy's mom and dad.

For Vo, meeting Trick and Lena had finally given him a direction for his protective instincts. His overprotective urges had all but faded, and I suspected he'd soon leave his body- guard job in favor of protecting his family full-time, even if all they needed protection from was long lines at the grocery store.

I didn't know how finding Elian would change me, or if it already had. All I knew was that whatever changes I had would be for the better.

"Earth to Alden? You there?" Memphis's voice broke into my thoughts, and I shook my head.

"Sorry. Lost in thought. What did you say?"

"I said Neel really wants to meet Elian. He was annoyed we went without him," Memphis repeated, and I winced.

"I should apologize to him," I said, but he waved me off.

"Nah, we chose not to bring him or Pax. Not your fault. We figured we were already breaking the rules. We didn't want to push Elian too much," he said, and I nodded.

"Maybe in a few days you could bring the boys?" I suggested, and he tapped the counter as he finished his drink.

"Sounds like a plan. Do you need to borrow the car? I dropped everyone off today, so it's still here."

"That would be great, thanks." If the meeting had been at Raiden's place, I could've just walked over, but the packland was on the other side of town, and even *I* wasn't going to walk all that way if I could drive instead.

I just hoped the meeting would be more productive than the Mistvale clan gatherings usually were.

Elian

After Alden left, I spent a few hours in my land, communicating with all the plants and resolving any issues that'd cropped up. Once that was done, I returned to my garden and changed into different clothes. Living in the human form required so much extra work, but I didn't mind.

At one point, I'd thought I would never feel comfortable, that I would never want to be in a human form. But I felt differently now.

Now, I wanted to talk to other people, to spend time with people whom I was starting to call friends. I wanted to go outside my park, to explore the town that had once been a part of my land.

Did I feel brave enough to do that? I'd planned to venture outside with Alden for the very first time, but what if I did something else?

What if I gave Alden a surprise? He'd done so much for me over the past few months, and I wanted to do something nice for him too.

I'd need help, though. I still didn't know where exactly Alden lived, and while I felt ready to go outside, I didn't know if I wanted to walk all that way.

Today was the perfect opportunity to try too, since Alden was at his meeting. I hadn't thought I'd be up for taking another step so soon, but meeting Alden's family had energized and motivated me rather than exhausting me the way I'd thought it would.

Taking my phone out of its spot, I scrolled through my contacts as I debated who to contact. Orion would be at the library right now, and I didn't want to bother him at work. Memphis, maybe? He should be home.

Me: Hey, Memphis. Are you free?

The 'typing' bubble popped up almost instantly, and I sat down on the ground to wait for his reply.

A rabbit snuck out of the bushes as I waited, and I smiled at the little furball as he slowly walked toward me.

I held my hand out, and he drew closer, pressing his nose to my skin and snuffling adorably.

My phone buzzed with a reply, but he paid it no mind.

Memphis: Yep. Did you get bored without Alden?

Me: In a way. I want to do something for Alden, and I was hoping for your help with it.

While I waited for his reply, I switched to the camera app and took a picture of the rabbit. Now that I had a phone of my own, I could see why humans were so obsessed with taking pictures of cute things. It was fun, and I wanted to show the picture to Alden later. Most of the animals at the park were still wary of anyone but me, so he hadn't seen them.

Memphis: Of course! What do you need help with?

Me: Well, I wanted to come to your place and surprise Alden when he returns.

I sent the text and then wondered if it sounded pathetic to Memphis. I was excited about the prospect of leaving what was basically my house.

Memphis: Oh, that sounds fun! Alden will be stunned. What do you need me to do?

I told him how I wasn't quite sure where to go and was hoping he could pick me up. I wished I didn't have to ask for his assistance, but I did not want to risk getting lost because I was too prideful to ask for help. That would be just dumb.

Memphis: Oof. Alden took the car to the meeting, so I can't pick you up personally, but I can get one of the others to do it, if you're okay with that.

Me: I don't want to be too much trouble.

Memphis: Trust me. Vo will be happy to help.

Me: Then I'd truly appreciate his help. Should I text him?

Memphis: Nah, leave it to me. Expect him to be there in 30.

Me: Okay. Thank you so much.

Memphis: My pleasure, Elian. Would you please stay long enough to meet Neel?

I blinked at his question, surprised at the request. Then again, I shouldn't be all that shocked considering what Memphis said yesterday.

Me: I'd love to.

Memphis: Great. I'll see you soon.

With a sigh, I locked my phone and gave the rabbit one last scratch behind his ear before getting up.

I dusted off my pants—seriously, clothes could be so cumbersome—and stuck my phone in a pocket before digging out a basket and heading to my orchard. I was going to Alden's —and Memphis and Orion's—house for the first time, so I should bring something. What better gift than fresh fruits?

After I'd filled one basket, I remembered what Trick had said yesterday and grabbed another one for him and Vo. I had to thank him for driving me anyway, so this was the perfect way to do it.

With two baskets of fruits, I headed toward the entrance of the park, sending waves of magic into the land as I walked.

I'd never been away from my land before, and I didn't know how long I'd be able to stay. I knew as a fact that dryads could do it without hurting, but I'd never put it to the test until now. What if you had to build up tolerance to do that?

The sound of a car driving up pulled me out of my thoughts, and I peeked outside to find Vo waiting for me. He waved when he spotted me, and I smiled at him before I slowly took my first step outside the park.

I held my breath as I did it, but when nothing happened, I took another step and then another and then another until I was at the car.

Vo leaned across to open my door for me, and then took the fruit baskets from my hands and put them in the space in front of the backseat.

"Hey, Elian," Vo greeted me with a wide smile as I got in, and then helped me put on the seatbelt. He must've guessed this was my first time in a car.

"Hey, Vo. Thank you so much for helping me," I said, gripping the handle on the door as he started driving.

"It's no problem. Trick's with Lena, so I'm going to stick around for a bit. I want to see Alden's reaction when he sees you," he said with a grin, and I shook my head at the excitement on his face. Alden's friends might just have been more excited than me.

"That's great. I'm a little nervous about leaving, but I think I'll be fine," I said, and Vo shot me a wink before turning his focus on the road.

At least, I hope I will be.

TWENTY-ONE

Alden

Arriving at the packland, I was met by Noel at the door, who told me he'd switched with Tate at the homeschool so he could attend the meeting. I hadn't been aware he'd be joining us, but I was glad for it. Noel was one of the earliest members of the clan, and he was always helpful during important discussions.

"Come on, everyone's in the Gathering Hall," Noel said, and I glanced down at him with a wince.

"Shit, am I late?"

"Nah, you're fine. They all just showed up early."

Exhaling in relief, I followed him to the cabin we'd dubbed the Gathering Hall. It consisted of just one huge room and a bunch of chairs, and it was where all the clan meetings were held, though the unofficial get-togethers usually happened in Noel's backyard.

"Hey, Alden," Raphael called the moment I stepped into the room, and I waved at him before checking who else was here.

Rebba, the shifter pack's alpha, was there, along with Caleb, Noel's mate and Rebba's second. Raiden was there, of course, and then there was Raphael. Raphael didn't hold any official position, but like Noel, he was one of the earliest members of the clan.

"Come on, let's get this party—uh, I mean, meeting started," Raphael said, and I shook my head as I took one of the empty chairs and Noel took the other. Someone—my bet was Raphael—had set the chairs in a circle, and I felt more like I was at group therapy than in a meeting.

"So, today's meeting was originally supposed to be about the growing supe population and declining human population in Mistvale," Raiden said, and I narrowed my eyes at the 'supposed to be.' Did that mean the agenda of the meeting had changed now?

"But since that was decided," Raiden said, and I turned my attention to his words instead of my own thoughts. "Things have changed. Someone—a vampire—recently tried to buy the Silent Creek Park. We stopped him since the park belongs to a dryad, but his intentions weren't bad. I've made sure to vet every supe who moves into Mistvale with both magical and non-magical means, and Calix passed all conditions. His intention with the park had been to build an apartment complex for supes so more of us could live here."

"That's not a bad idea," Raphael mused, and Raiden nodded at him.

"I agree. I promised Calix I'd help him find a suitable land and shape the complex, and I intend to keep it."

"You'd need a lot of land for a project like that. And money," I said, and Raiden waved me off like only someone with too much cash could.

"Money's not an issue, and we think we might have a solution for the land," he said, then glanced over at Noel.

"Yep, my turn. So, the organization that employs me and owns this land wants to sell it. Most of the Christmas trees we grow here are shipped out, and they recently acquired some land that is much closer to their shipping routes, so they want to sell this one since it's no longer profitable," Noel explained, and my brows shot up.

The Christmas tree farm was a staple of Mistvale, and the pack lived on the farm's land in exchange for taking care of it. What would happen to the pack if they sold the land?

"So you're thinking of building the complex here?" Raphael demanded, his voice high with disbelief.

"Not here exactly," Raiden corrected. "The land where the trees are right now is large enough for what we need. They've already stopped planting new saplings, so after Christmas this year, that land will be free to use."

"And this place? What would happen to the pack's land? The cabins? The mini-shelter?" Raphael asked, echoing the questions running through my head.

"They will all be right here," Rebba said, piping in for the first time.

"But how? I mean, as long as the land is owned by someone else, won't there always be the risk of losing it somehow?" I asked, and Raiden smiled at me.

"Which is exactly why it won't be owned by someone else. *I* will be buying the land from Noel's employers, and then I'll contract Calix to build the complex. Or, if he wants to do it himself, I can sell him only enough land for his project...along with a few conditions, of course."

I shook my head in wonder, stunned by Raiden's quick thinking. The man had created a foolproof plan practically all on his own. I guessed that was his dragon brain hard at work.

"Okay. Looks like you have it all figured out, dragon daddy," Raphael said, and I snorted a laugh.

"Stop calling me that," Raiden growled at him, but Raphael merely grinned.

"No chance. You always react so perfectly," he teased, and then sent a flying kiss Raiden's way.

Shaking his head, Raiden seemed to decide the best way to deal with Raph was to ignore him. Turning to me, he said, "What do you think, Alden? Would it work? Or is there something I'm missing?"

Knowing exactly what he was asking me, I closed my eyes and focused on my gut as I thought about the plan he'd laid out.

Unlike a witch's potion or a warlock's spell, my magic wasn't exact. It was a bunch of feelings all jumbled up together, feelings that I had to parse through to make sense of exactly what it was telling me.

Sometimes, it was easy to figure out what it meant, while other times I didn't have the faintest idea of what it might be trying to say.

Right then, though, I could tell exactly what it was.

"It'll work. It might even benefit everyone," I said finally, and Raiden gave a smile of utter satisfaction as he sat back in his chair.

"How?" Noel asked curiously, and I sighed.

"That, I have no clue about," I declared, and Raphael let out a laugh.

"I really like your power, Alden. It's so fun and mysterious," he said, and I accepted the compliment with a mock-bow.

"What about the other topic? The changing demographic of Mistvale?" Caleb, the only person who'd stayed silent this whole time, asked, and all eyes turned to Raiden once more.

"Honestly, there's nothing we can do to change things in any way, but I can assure you that I've carefully vetted every new resident we've had in the past few years. Right now, the supes versus the humans not in the know seems to be a 70/30 split, and at the rate it's been changing, Mistvale could become a supe-only town within the next five to seven years if there aren't any complications."

"That soon?" I asked, surprised. While I'd known about the changes happening around us, I'd still thought it would be years—a decade, at least—before that happened.

Raiden nodded, and his storm-gray eyes met each of ours one by one. "When that happens, we'll need to figure out the next steps. We could cut Mistvale off completely from the humans, or we could let it stay just the way it is now. Whatever we decide to do, we have time to think it through."

Everyone was silent for the next few minutes, probably digesting the bombshell Raiden had just dropped.

"Wow, that's some serious stuff to think about. How about we end this meeting here, stew on everything we've learned, and get back together some other time? Five years may not seem that long to us, but it's still a while away," Raphael said, showing off that wise side of himself that he usually hid under his goofy exterior.

"Raph's right. Let's stop here and we can talk again once we have some solid ideas," Raiden said, and just like that, the meeting concluded.

I stuck around to chat for a few minutes, but soon I was back in the car and on my way home. I'd need to drop the car, but after that, I was heading right back to the park. To Elian.

Elian

I was a bundle of nerves as I waited for Alden to get here. Memphis had assured me he'd come here first to drop off the car, and that, seeing Vo's car outside, he'd come in to say hi.

Vo had suggested I open the door and greet him when he got here, but Memphis had shot down the idea because they might miss his reaction if he was still outside. If I wasn't so nervous, I'd be amused by how excited those two were.

"Quill is going to be so mad he missed this," Vo said with a grin, and Memphis rolled his eyes.

"It's his fault for going and getting himself a normal, human job," Memphis said, and Vo raised a brow at him.

"You're a bartender," he reminded, as if Memphis might've forgotten.

"I work at night. Like a good supe," Memphis said, and I bit back a chuckle at their argument. "And supes drink alcohol too."

"Well, supes drive cars too, so I don't know why we're arguing about this," Vo shot back, and Memphis growled before flopping down beside me on the couch. After a lifetime of sitting on wood and grass, the cushiony couch felt too soft to me, but it was nice too. Like sitting on a cloud.

"You know, this is a very sweet thing you're doing for Alden. I'm glad he found you," Memphis said, his voice turning soft and sincere as he met my eyes.

For an incubus, Memphis kept his powers checked pretty well. Usually, even being in the same room with an incubus pulled a person toward them, made them want to please the incubus, but I felt practically no different even though he was so close to me that our arms were touching.

"I'm glad for that too," I said when I remembered what he'd said. "I feel like before Alden found me, I was...stuck. Doing the same thing every day and believing that was all my life would ever be. Alden changed that, and I'm grateful for it."

"I know what you mean," Memphis said softly, and his eyes flicked forward. I followed his gaze to a set of framed pictures, one with the whole gang, their mates, and the kids, and another with just Memphis, Orion, and their sons, Neel and Pax.

"He's here!" Vo said as he shot to his feet, and our introspection ended as all the nerves I'd managed to push back returned in full force. I wasn't even sure what exactly I was worried about. I knew Alden would only react positively to my presence, and I knew this was going to be a great surprise for him. What was I so anxious about?

"Okay, okay, he's coming up," Vo said, then skipped away from the window to stand on the other side of the room, a spot with a perfect vantage point, I assumed.

The door opened, and I held my breath as Alden stepped inside and closed the door behind him, his eyes focused on his phone.

"Memphis? Vo?" he called, and my phone buzzed in my pocket a second before Alden glanced up and spotted me.

His eyes went wide, and he blinked slowly as he stared at me before taking three huge steps that had our chests pressing together.

"Elian," he breathed, his eyes roaming all over my face as if he wanted to make sure it was really me. "What are you...how?" he demanded, then shook his head and turned his gaze on Vo.

"You brought Elian here?" he asked, and Vo shrugged.

"He asked for a lift, so I gave him one."

Alden turned his focus back to me, his eyes still a little wide.

"I wanted to surprise you," I said by way of explanation, and he laughed softly.

"You've surprised me, all right. You can't imagine how happy I am to see you here, Pan," he murmured, and I grinned widely.

"Pan?" I heard Memphis mumble behind me, but I ignored him in favor of rising up on my toes to kiss Alden.

"Damn it. I didn't need to see that!" Vo complained, and Alden smiled against my lips.

"Eh, I'm always up for a snack. This is the first time I'm getting some from Alden, though. Huh," Memphis said, and it took me a minute to realize what he meant. Memphis was an incubus, and incubi fed on arousal. While I had no desire to act on it, I did feel physically aroused when I kissed Alden. Cheeks flushing with warmth, I quickly pulled away from Alden.

"Did you *have* to say that?" Alden demanded, glaring daggers at Memphis, who shrugged.

"Sorry, Elian. Didn't mean to fluster you," he said with a smile at me, before glancing at Alden.

"Vo and I are going to head over to his for a bit, but I'll be back with Orion and the boys later," Memphis told him before turning to me. "You still up for meeting the boys?"

I nodded quickly, and he smiled. "Perfect. See you too later, then. Come on, Pipsqueak."

I raised a brow at the nickname, and Vo growled at him, but followed him to the door nonetheless. Once they'd left, Alden raised a brow at me.

"So, what would you like to do now?" he asked, and I answered quickly because I already knew exactly what I wanted.

"I would like to see your room."

TWENTY-TWO

Alden

Walking into my house and finding Elian waiting for me there had been a monumental shock. It'd also felt a little jarring, like two pieces of my world had collided into one another. But once the surprise was gone, all that was left was excitement and happiness.

"Of course. It's upstairs," I said, and took Elian's hand before leading him up.

"Do you know this is the first time I've been in a house? At least one with modern amenities," Elian said, and I glanced at him.

"Really?"

"Yeah. A long time ago, a human invited me into his hut, and that was the only time."

"You never thought of building something for yourself?"

"Nah. At my core, I'm part of Mother Nature. Trees and rivers don't need protection from the sun or the wind or the rain, so why should I? As long as I'm in my true form, those things don't affect me. And even in my human form, rain would only make me wet. I don't mind getting wet," he said with a shrug, and I smiled at his declaration. It made sense too, if I didn't think about him as just a person. He was something much bigger, a being of nature tasked with nurturing and protecting the land he called home.

"Here we are," I said as we stepped inside my room, and Elian let go of my hand so he could look around. I waited patiently as he flitted about the room, humming to himself as he examined my various possessions.

I didn't have many, to be honest. I liked having a roomy space, so other than my desk, dresser, and bed, I didn't have any other furniture in my room. I did have a lot of little trinkets on my desk, things I'd collected over the years, and that was what had pulled Elian's attention.

"These are cute, and pretty too. Do they all have a story behind them?" he asked, picking up a small ceramic kettle with cat ears.

"Some of them, yeah. Some I just picked up because they looked cute. It's an indulgence of mine," I explained, adjusting my glasses.

"The pirate's loot, huh?" he teased, and I rolled my eyes at him.

"Your room's nice. Very open. It needs some greenery, though," he said, and I chuckled.

"Yeah? What would you recommend?" I asked, and he circled around the room, probably scouting out the best spots for me to keep plants in.

"Maybe a few potted wildflower bushes? Some begonias, pink ones would look great. You know what? I'll grow some plants for you in the garden, and you can bring some pots to transfer them into," he said, and I smiled at the passionate look on his face. I also didn't hate the idea of having plants he'd grown with his magic in my room.

"Aye, aye, captain," I said, giving him a salute, and he grinned.

"You're the pirate, remember?" he said, and I shook my head.

After he'd examined the room to his heart's content, Elian walked over to my bed and climbed onto it before sitting cross-legged on the duvet.

"Wow, this bed is even softer than the couch. How did you ever manage to sleep on the ground with me?" Elian demanded, and I chuckled as I joined him.

"Well, you were there," I reminded him, and he smiled and ducked his head to avoid my gaze.

"Can I ask you a question?" I asked, remembering a random thought I'd had during the meeting.

"Of course."

"The magic you use now to keep humans out of your par k...couldn't you have used it before? When all of Mistvale was your land?" I asked, and Elian pursed his lips.

"I could have. I mean, my powers come from my land, so the bigger my land, the more powerful I am. But the way my magic works right now is that it repels humans by making them change their mind or forget where they were going. It only affects them if they get close enough to the park with the intention of going inside."

"So, if someone's walking by, they'll see the park, but if they want to go inside, they won't?"

"No, they'll still see the park. They'll just forget they were headed there or change their mind," he clarified.

"So they think they want to visit the town, but then change their mind or forget every time. It isn't too suspicious for a place this small, but if it was a whole town, things would be a lot different, and after a while, the humans would've realized they never get around to checking out the new land, and they would've grown suspicious. Does that make sense?"

"It does, yeah," I said as I digested everything he'd said. "It's like skimming the cash from the register versus robbing a bank."

Elian raised a brow at me. "Well, thanks for comparing it to a crime, but yes, something like that. When they tried to take my land, I could've fought. I was supposed to fight. I could've destroyed anyone—human or supe—who tried. I was powerful enough. But I didn't want to spill blood on my land, so instead I retreated. I gave the humans the space they needed to build their land in exchange for them leaving me in peace in my little slice of land. And for a few generations, they did."

"But then they forgot the old stories, and you had to put up the ward," I surmised, and he nodded.

"Exactly."

"How do you feel right now? Being away from your land?" I asked, and he tilted his head side to side, as if examining his emotions.

"Not too bad. I think some part of me recognizes this land used to be mine, so I don't feel too out of sorts."

"You know, you could claim this land again, once Mistvale is a supes-only town," I suggested, and his brows shot up.

"How would I do that?"

"I don't know how your magic works, to be honest. But despite the buildings, Mistvale still has a healthy share of flora, right? And if you did control it, you could decide where someone could or couldn't build new things," I said, and then wondered where this idea had come from. Was it my magic at work or just my wish that Elian didn't have to be locked up in the park most of the time?

"I don't know if I *can* do that, but it doesn't sound bad," Elian said finally, and I smiled.

"Imagine that. A town where the land is controlled by a dryad and the sky is owned by a dragon. Now that's what I'd call a supernatural haven."

Elian

Over the next few hours, Alden and I chatted about any topic that came to mind. He told me all about the meeting, about Raiden's estimate for when Mistvale would become a supe-only town, about their plan to build the apartment complex on the land that currently housed the Christmas tree farm.

Building where the farm was wasn't the same as destroying my park because those trees were meant to be cut down. They were grown with a different magic, one that gave them the opportunity to experience joy and fulfillment by bringing happiness to the homes of people. For those trees, not being cut down would've been a worse fate, and I understood that. I also knew that the elf who took care of that farm made sure that no tree was truly hurt when he cut them. He'd come to my park a few times, and my trees and I could feel how much he cared about Mother Nature and all her kids. I liked him, even if I'd never actually met him.

Our conversation switched from one topic to another with an ease that came from spending the past few months talking to each other every day. I'd never felt as comfortable talking to anyone as I did with Alden, which was probably why, in a lull in our conversation, I found myself speaking words that I probably should've saved for a special moment.

"Alden, I love you," I said, surprising us both. He recovered first, and a wide smile replaced the look of surprise on his face.

"That was completely out of the blue, but I don't care. I love you too, Elian."

Maybe the moment didn't need to be special to say the words. Maybe saying the words was all that was needed to make the moment special.

"Sorry, I just had to," I said sheepishly. My feelings for Alden had grown so slowly and steadily that I hadn't realized just how all-encompassing they'd become until the words spilled out from my lips. I'd started feeling something for Alden the day he left me that very first cupcake, and it'd only grown from then on.

"I don't mind at all. I'm glad you said it," Alden said, reaching out to brush his fingertips against my cheek.

In our position, others might've proceeded to have sex to celebrate, but that wasn't something either of us were interested in. But I knew exactly what we could do.

"Come here," I said, taking Alden's hand and tugging him toward the center of the bed.

Lying down, I patted the space beside me, and Alden lay down, a curious look on his face.

Turning on my side, I curled up close to him, and he got the message instantly. Alden wrapped his arm around me, linked our legs together , and pressed a kiss to the top of my head.

"Mmm, perfect," I declared, and he chuckled softly. "I never realized being held could feel so good."

"Holding you in my arms feels pretty good too," Alden said, his voice hushed and full of sweetness.

"Let's do a lot more of it then, okay?" I said, and he squeezed me closer to him.

"Sounds good to me."

We lay like that for a while. It could've been a few minutes or a few hours, I wouldn't know. I drifted somewhere between sleep and wakefulness, and I only came back to the land of the living when there was a knock at the door.

"Hey, we're back. The boys are downstairs, so come down whenever. We're making hot chocolate," Memphis's voice came through the door.

"What's hot chocolate?" I asked, and Alden's eyes went wide.

"I can't believe I never brought you hot chocolate. Come on. You need to try it," he said as he hurried upright, and I followed after him, a little puzzled, a little amused.

"Is it really that good?" I asked as I followed him to the door, and he scoffed.

"That good? It's the best thing the witches ever came up with," he said, and I tilted my head, confused.

"I thought it was a human food."

"It is now, but witches were the first ones to brew both hot chocolate and coffee, just like they were the first ones to brew tea. Humans just didn't know that they were witches."

We'd reached the kitchen by the time Alden had finished explaining, and Memphis spoke before I could.

"Is he telling you the story of how hot chocolate was first made?" Memphis asked with a raised brow, and I smiled. "Figured as much. He loves that one."

"It's a good story!" Alden exclaimed, and I chuckled.

That was when I spotted the two heads peeking at me from behind Orion, who was standing at the stove and presumably making this fabled hot chocolate.

"Oh, hello! You must be Neel and Pax. I'm Elian," I said, waving my hand in greeting.

The boy with light blue eyes stepped around Orion first, and I guessed he was Neel.

"Hey, Elian! It's nice to meet you. Dad's told us a lot about you," Neel said, and I smiled self-consciously. It was becoming very clear to me very quickly that I had to idea how to communicate with a child, and I glanced at Alden for help, hoping he could read the look on my face.

"All right, hot chocolate's ready. Everyone, grab a mug and get in line!" Orion said, saving me from trying to figure out what to say.

Everyone hurried over to the cabinets to hunt for a mug, and I watched with a smile as Alden leaned down to whisper something in Pax's ear.

A moment later, Pax rushed off, and I continued watching Alden as he moved around the room sharing words with everyone, completely at ease.

A tug on my shirt made me look down, and I found Pax standing beside me, two empty mugs in his hand. He held one out to me, and my eyes widened as I slowly took it from him.

"For me? Thank you," I said, giving him a wide smile. He gave me a small grin in return before rushing off toward Neel, and I glanced up to find Alden watching me.

He winked, and I felt butterflies flutter in my belly. God, I was one lucky dryad.

TWENTY-THREE

Alden

Watching Elian interact and spend time with my family would never get old. The fact that we were doing it in the house instead of the park made me even happier.

Not because I felt more at home here than at the park, but because the fact that Elian was here showed me just how much work he was putting in our relationship.

Had I done the same? Sure, I'd visited Elian at the park as much as I could, but beyond that, what had I truly done?

Elian had overturned his whole life to make space for me in it, and I was pretty much the same as I'd been before I met him. I wanted to do something for Elian, to show him my dedication to him, to us.

Elian laughed at something Memphis had said, and I found myself smiling even though I hadn't heard a word of what they were talking about.

What could I do to show Elian my commitment to him?

A date, I realized with a start. It wasn't enough, but it was surely a good starting point. While we spent every day together, we hadn't been on a single date, at least not officially.

Maybe I could plan something for Elian, take him somewhere that was outside the park but still remote enough that it wouldn't make him too anxious.

Yeah, that was what I was going to do. A nice evening out for Elian and me, where we could eat, talk, and just be. It didn't sound much different than what we already did, but I was going to do my best to make it a unique experience for Elian.

"What thoughts are you lost in?" Memphis said, nudging my leg with his, and I focused on the present, putting my planning on hold for the moment.

"This is delicious," Elian said, and I grinned, ignoring Memphis's question in favor of replying to Elian.

"Isn't it? I told you so," I said, and he shook his head, a fond smile on his lips.

"Yes, you did. Shame on me for doubting you," he said, and I grinned.

"You're both very cute together," Neel said, and we blinked at each other before turning to look at him. I was sure my cheeks were red as the strawberries Elian grew. "What? You are!" Neel insisted when he saw the look we were giving him.

"I think they're just embarrassed, kiddo," Orion explained, and I thanked him mentally. At least Neel had one competent dad, because Memphis was too busy laughing his ass off to do much else.

"What's there to be embarrassed about? Love is supposed to be good, right? Why would it be embarrassing?" Neel asked with the innocence only a child could have. Honestly, no matter what I said, Memphis had done a great job raising him, and Orion and Pax's addition to their family had only made things better.

"You're right, Neel. I was being an idiot. Love is nothing to be embarrassed or ashamed about," I said, sharing a smile with Elian. "You're a smart one, kiddo."

Neel grinned at me before taking a sip of his hot chocolate, and I knew he'd grow up to be a kind, sweet man who'd do great things. He'd soaked up the best qualities of all of us, after all.

After we'd finished our hot chocolate, Orion convinced Elian to stay for dinner, and I shot him a smile. He was a big part of why Elian felt comfortable around everyone.

Orion had helped Elian in the beginning, helped him by becoming his friend and confidant. Without his help, I didn't Elian would've been able to be so brave so soon. I was grateful for everything Orion had done—and was still doing—for Elian. I needed to get him a present for all his help. Maybe a first edition of one of his favorite books? He had quite a collection himself, though, so I'd need to be creative.

"You're vegan, right?" Memphis asked, and Elian nodded quickly.

"Yes. But please don't feel like you have to eat vegan for my sake," he said, and Memphis waved him off.

"It's fine. I won't die without cheese for one night. Or at least I hope I won't," he said with a wink, making Elian laugh.

Conversation flowed easily as Orion and Memphis made dinner with Neel and Pax acting like little assistants. I wasn't much of a cook, but unlike Vo, I was completely okay with it, preferring to stay out of the kitchen and let the competent ones work. I did my part of the chores, though, because I wanted to pull my weight in the house.

Once dinner was ready, we all sat around the dining table passing the dishes and gobbling up the food. Everything Orion and Memphis had made was delicious, and I told them as much.

"It truly is. Alden has been introducing me to a lot of human food recently, and this is one of the best dishes I've had so far," Elian concurred, and Orion smiled.

"Let me guess. The only dishes to surpass this are what Trick made," Memphis guessed, and Elian laughed.

"Yes, you're right. I really enjoyed the spiciness of his food."

"Vo did a good job finding a master chef for his mate," Memphis joked, and I rolled my eyes.

"Yes, because that's exactly why they're mates," I dead-panned. "So you can get all the delicious Indian food you want."

Memphis shrugged as he stuffed another spoonful of pasta into his mouth. Orion had created a lentil-based sauce that was just the right amount of spicy and filling, and I didn't want to stop eating despite how stuffed I was starting to feel.

We stayed at the table until everyone had finished, and then Elian and I insisted on cleaning up since they'd done all the cooking.

I washed the dishes while Elian dried them, and soon enough, we'd cleaned everything up. Orion had tidied the counter as he cooked, so there wasn't much to do there, and we returned to the living room once the kitchen was spotless again.

Orion and Memphis were both seated on the couch when we got there, with Neel and Pax leaning into them on either side. They looked stuffed and sleepy as all hell, and I gave them five minutes before they started dozing off.

Elian

We helped Orion and Memphis put Neel and Pax to bed—they'd fallen asleep on the couch and had to be carried to bed. I also learned a new term called *food coma*—and then returned to the living room. It had gotten dark outside quite a while ago, and sometime in the last hour, I'd started itching to go back to the park.

"You're welcome to stay the night, Elian," Memphis said, and I glanced over at Alden, who took one look at my face and shook his head.

"Nah, we'd better go back. We've been away for a while," he said, and I mentally thanked him for his assist. I didn't want to be rude by declining the invitation, but I also didn't think I could stay away from the park much longer.

"All right, no worries. But now that we know you can leave, we'll expect regular visits, okay?" Memphis said, and I smiled as I nodded. I'd enjoyed spending time with them, and I'd also enjoyed being in this home. I wouldn't mind coming back.

"Would you like me to drive you?" Orion asked, and Alden and I shared another glance before declining. It was surprising how easily I could read Alden now. Was that the result of all the time we'd spent together?

"The weather looks good tonight, so we'll take a stroll," Alden said, and Orion smiled.

"That sounds like a good idea."

They walked us to the door and then waved us off. Alden slid his hand into mine, linking our fingers together, and we started walking.

While there were some people on the streets—almost all of them supes—it wasn't very crowded, and I assumed it was because it was what Alden called a 'work night.'

"Wait, doesn't Memphis work nights?" I asked as the thought struck, and Alden smiled at me.

"He does, but he took the evening off. Perks of being good friends with the boss, I suppose."

"So his boss is a supe too?" I asked, and Alden hummed.

"His name is Jules, and he's a mermaid-siren. Really sweet guy," Alden said, and I nodded. I think I might've seen him around the park once or twice, though I couldn't be sure.

"Hey, I had a thought," Alden said a few moments later, and I made a questioning sound as I moved closer to him.

While I didn't usually feel cold or heat, being in my human form so consistently seemed to have made me a little more sensitive, and Alden was extremely warm. It was like my body was being pulled to him without input from my brain.

"You know how we talked about you claiming the land of the whole town? If you did that, how exactly would you go about it?" Alden asked, and I blinked, surprised. That wasn't what I'd been expecting him to ask.

"Oh. Well, first I'd go into my land, and then I'd let my magic flow out. Once it reached outside the confines of my land, I'd use it to ask every tree, every plant and critter it encountered if they would accept my guardianship. I can give them a boost as an example of what I can offer them, but I can only extend my reach to them if they say yes. Did that make sense?" I'd never had to put my process into words, and I was starting to realize it wasn't very easy. I'd had a hard time explaining my anti-human shield earlier too.

"So you can't forcefully take land, huh?" Alden asked after a moment, and I shook my head.

"I would never do that even if I could. But I can't."

"Well, that's a bit unfair, isn't it? If humans can take your land by force, shouldn't you be able to do the same?"

"Then what would be the difference between us?" I asked, shaking my head. "Those plants and trees are razed down without a word by the humans. I'm not going to assume control of them in the same way."

Alden was quiet for a moment, and I wondered if I'd spoken too harshly. I'd been trying to be honest, but could I have put things a little differently?

Alden stopped walking suddenly, and turned to face me, using his grip on my hand to tug me close. He wrapped his free arm around my torso, leaned forward, and pressed a soft kiss on my forehead. "You're a wonderful person, Elian," he said in a voice so soft the breeze almost blew his words away before I could hear them.

My cheeks heated up under his praise, and I rested my head on his chest, wrapping my own free arm around him to return the hug. Alden felt amazing against me, warm and firm, my pillar of support.

"Come on, my sweet Pan. Let's get you back to your park before you turn into a pumpkin," Alden said, and I pulled back to frown up at him.

"Pumpkin?" I asked, unsure if I should be amused or offended.

Alden's eyes widened, and then he gave a laugh. "Looks like we need to watch *Cinderella* one of these days," he said, and I surmised that it'd been a reference to some movie or show. He should know better than to think I'd get those.

The rest of our walk was spent in silence, and I enjoyed every moment of it. The weather felt like it was turning, like it'd start raining soon, but I didn't care. Alden's hand was wrapped firmly around mine, and our sides were close enough that I could feel his heat. We were nearing the park now, and the streets were all but empty in this area.

"If Mistvale does turn into a supe-only town, would you walk around here in your true form?" I asked, glancing up at Alden, and he frowned.

"I don't know. I don't think so. Being in my true form around people I don't know...it's unnerving. Maybe I'd be able to do it at the packland, surrounded by the clan. But out here? I don't think so."

"That's okay. They don't deserve to see your beautiful form anyway," I said with a wave of my hand, and he turned his gaze on me, one brow raised.

"Are you saying I'm not beautiful in this form?" he asked, and my eyes widened.

"No, of course not!" I said quickly, and he grinned. "You jerk!" I smacked his shoulder in annoyance, and he laughed as he jumped away, though he still hadn't let go of my hand, so he could only move so far.

"Sorry! I just had to," he said with a cute little smile, and I rolled my eyes.

"Sure you did."

The moment we reached the park, I hurried through the entrance, dragging Alden behind me. Relief washed through me as I stepped inside, and I could feel the way the flora cheered up at my return.

"Feel better?" Alden asked softly, and I nodded.

Smiling, he leaned forward and kissed me, and in a matter of seconds, everything felt right once again.

TWENTY-FOUR

Alden

There was no way the plan could go wrong, but I was still a bundle of nerves and excitement as I returned to the park the next day. I'd gone back earlier to shower and change clothes, and then I'd made a pit-stop at Vo's—waking him and Trick in the process, which I'd apologized profusely for—to talk to Trick about my plan and if it would even be possible. He'd assured me he'd make it work, and I'd left their place feeling a lot more at ease about my plan.

The walk to the park had given me more than enough time to worry, though, and now my mind was filled with all the things that could go wrong.

I wanted this date to be perfect for Elian, and I was going to do everything in my power to make sure it would be.

"You're back!" Elian exclaimed as I stepped into the clearing, and I smiled the second I spotted him sitting cross-legged on the ground. It was an instinctual reaction now, and needed no input from my brain.

"Oh. Who's that?" I said when I spotted a ball of brown fur peeking out from behind his leg.

"We became friends the other day. I think he came from the woods and decided to stay here," Elian said.

"So animals can choose to join your land even without your input?" I asked, and Elian hummed.

"Sort of. They can live here without me knowing. Like, I don't know all the bugs and bees that live in my park right now. But once I see them or sense them on one of my check-ups, I can make sure I take care of them. Or, if they eat one of the plants I've been nurturing, that connects them to me."

"Wow, it's all so...fascinating," I said, unable to find a more apt word. Elian's magic was so intriguing, and someday, I wanted to know every little detail of how it worked. I had to admit, though, that right then the sole reason behind my questions was that I didn't want Elian to realize how nervous I was, especially since our date wasn't until this evening.

"Will it let me touch it?" I asked curiously as I took a step closer to Elian and the rabbit.

"Why don't you give it a try?" he asked, brushing the pads of his fingers over the rabbit's back.

Nodding, I cautiously drew closer to Elian before sitting on the ground in front of him in a pose similar to his. The rabbit was still stuck to his side, and I offered it my hand. It waited a few moments before taking a step forward to sniff at it, and I smiled as I shared a glance with Elian.

"Here," he said, handing me small, broken-off pieces of cabbage. "I grew a patch for him," he said with a sheepish smile when I gave him a questioning look, and I grinned as I returned my attention to the rabbit. Of course he'd grown a patch of cabbage for the rabbit. I wasn't surprised in the least.

I offered a leaf to the rabbit in the middle of my palm, and his nose went into overdrive as he caught scent of it. I grinned as he gobbled it off right from my palm, and then slowly fed him the rest of the pieces.

Once he was satisfied, he hopped on away to wherever he'd created his hidey-hole, and I wiped my hands on my pants before turning my attention to Elian. "Do you have many small friends like him around?"

"Some," he said with a shrug. "But they die too quickly for me to get truly attached." That sounded so sad, and the look on Elian's face told me he did get attached even with their short lifespans.

Taking his hand in mine, I squeezed softly. "Their life is much nicer because of you. I bet they all love you to bits."

Elian smiled at my words, and my chest went all warm and tingly. I didn't think I'd ever get used to how good it felt to make Elian smile. It filled me with a sense of accomplishment, like I'd won some great war. It was a fanciful notion, but I enjoyed it nonetheless.

After a lunch of a variety of fruits, Elian and I spent a few hours talking about all the other things he could grow in his garden to add some variety to our food options. I, of course, suggested the idea of offering Trick a regular supply of freshly grown veggies in return for deliciously cooked vegan food, but Elian shot me down. He'd happily supply produce to Trick, but he wasn't going to ask for anything.

By the time evening rolled around, I'd almost forgotten about our date. Almost. At five to six, my phone pinged with a text I'd been expecting, and I pulled it out of my pocket to check.

Trick: We're all set here. Come on by whenever.

Perfect. I glanced up at Elian, who was sitting across from me on the log with his phone between us. I'd been showing him the wonders of board games with a Snake & Ladders game on it.

"Is everything okay?"

"Hmm? Oh yes. Actually," I said, shifting in my seat as my nerves returned in full force. "I planned a date for us. For tonight."

"A date?" Elian asked, a hint of surprise in his voice.

"Yeah. It's outside, but I swear there won't be a lot of people around," I said, and Elian stared at me thoughtfully.

"Dates are an important part of a relationship, aren't they?" he asked, and I blinked. Not what I'd expected him to say, but I answered anyway.

"Yeah, they are, I suppose."

"Then I'd love to go on a date with you," he said with a smile, and I slumped in relief.

"Perfect. We should get ready, then," I said, and he glanced down at himself.

"Do I need to put on different clothes?" he asked, and I eyed his outfit. He was wearing a comfy hoodie—apparently, Elian ran a little cold in human form—and slim jeans, and I might've last seen his shoes in the garden. He hated wearing those since they disconnected him from his land.

"You feel comfortable, don't you?" I asked, and he nodded. "Then you don't need to change. You will have to wear shoes, though."

"I know," he grumbled softly, and I chuckled.

"Come on. We should get going."

Elian

Instead of walking, Alden had borrowed Memphis's car again, or, rather, they'd dropped it off at the park after they'd picked up the kids. I was always a little in awe of how much Alden's family did for each other. He was a lucky man to have a family that good, and I supposed so was I since I was a part of that now.

When Alden stopped driving, I realized we were in the commercial side of town. I'd never been this way before—not that that was saying much—but all the lit-up signboards told me exactly where we were.

I peeked out the window and realized we were parked in front of a restaurant. I turned to Alden, curious and a little worried. "A restaurant? I thought you said there won't be many people around."

"Trust me, Elian. I won't break my promise," Alden said, and I nodded slowly. I did trust Alden, and I believed him.

We got out of the car, and a man took the car keys from Alden before walking over to the car and getting inside.

I felt a little calmer when Alden took my hand in his and squeezed, and I followed him up the few stairs and into the restaurant. Into the very *empty* restaurant.

I glanced around the place, confused out of my mind. The lights were on, though they weren't too bright, and there were lit candles and fresh flowers on every table. But other than that, the place was completely empty.

A sound made me jump, and I realized someone had stepped into the room from a side-door. It was a young man, dressed in a black vest, white shirt, and black pants. He had a nice smile, and he walked straight to us as if he hadn't even noticed there was nobody else in the place.

"Hello! I'm Jasper, and I'll be your server tonight. Which table would you like to sit at?" the man asked, and I was still too stunned to say anything, so I let Alden field the question.

"That corner table there looks good," Alden said, and I nodded without checking where he was pointing.

"Of course. Come on this way."

I automatically followed the man, Alden's hand still gripping mine, and I was further confused when Alden dropped my hand to pull my chair back for me. Did he think I couldn't do it myself?

Once we were seated, Jasper placed what he called 'drink menus' in front of us before disappearing from sight.

"Was this too much? Do you hate it?" Alden asked, finally pulling me out of my cloud of confusion.

"Hmm? No, I don't hate it. I'm just...confused. Is the restaurant closed today?" I asked, glancing around the empty room.

"Not exactly," Alden said, and I gave him a curious look. "I kind of booked the whole place. This is Trick's restaurant."

I blinked, surprised. I hadn't taken the time to read the name out front because I'd been so surprised by the whole restaurant thing.

"Oh. Wasn't it expensive?" I asked, and he shrugged as if it was no big deal.

"It was worth it," he said, and I shook my head. I didn't have any money of my own. I'd never needed it. But I imagined something like this cost a lot, and to think Alden did it all for me...

"Thank you. This is absolutely wonderful," I said, and he grinned.

"Wait till you try the food. Trick made a special menu for us," he said, and I smiled because of course he did. Hadn't I been just thinking how helpful Alden's family was? And here was another example.

Alden ordered drinks for us, since I was clueless about alcohol. He assured me that the wine he'd ordered wouldn't make me feel drunk, which was the only reason I'd agreed.

Once we had our drinks, Jasper disappeared again, and I took a cautious sip of the drink. It was fruity, and not bad at all.

"You like it, don't you?" Alden asked with a smug smile, and I nodded.

"You know my taste well," I complimented, and he tilted his head in acceptance before taking a sip of his own.

While we waited for our food—I was excited to see what Trick had cooked up for us—we chatted like we would if we were at the park, and I realized that it didn't matter where we were. I would always feel at ease when talking to Alden. I hoped it was the same for him.

"Damn, that smells good," Alden said when the warm fragrance of spices drifted through the empty room, and I dragged in a deep breath as my mouth watered. I'd come a long way from having no interest in human food, and it was all thanks to the cupcake Alden had introduced me to.

"Someday, I'd like to go to the place you get those cupcakes from," I said, and Alden smiled, taking the change of topic in stride.

"I'd love to take you there. The bakery's in a shopping center, so it's crowded most of the time, but we can figure something out, I'm sure," he said, and I believed him. After all, he'd bought out a whole restaurant full of tables for me.

Jasper returned then, his arms laden with dishes.

"Here we are, gentlemen. A steaming hot veg lababdar and four missi rotis. We also have veg biryani, which I'll bring by in a little while so it stays hot. Enjoy, and please call out if you need anything!" Jasper spoke as he set the dishes and served up some of the hot veggies and one roti on each of our plates before walking away.

I'd gotten good at eating Indian food since Alden brought it for the first time, so I broke off a piece of the roti and scooped up some of the veg lababdar as Alden did the same.

I hadn't been sure what to expect when Alden asked me out on this date, but it had already exceeded all my expectations.

TWENTY-FIVE

Alden

After a filling meal, Elian and I had strawberry ice cream—vegan, of course—for dessert. I'd thought Trick would come by to say hi, but apparently, he'd decided to leave us be.

Elian didn't want to stay any longer after we'd finished, mostly because he thought it was rude to hold up the tables if we didn't need them. It was still early enough that if they opened now, they would be able to serve the late dinner crowd.

Once back in the car, I drove us to my place, where I dropped the car key in its usual hiding spot.

"I like walking from your place to the park. It's a very peaceful route," Elian said, and I glanced over at him with a smile.

"Maybe we should walk this route more often, then," I said, and he hummed.

"I don't have a problem with that. I would enjoy learning more. Now that my world has grown beyond the confines of my park, I don't want it to stop," he said, and I squeezed his hand.

"Then it won't," I promised him, and he smiled up at me.

"You should bring some of your clothes over, though. So you don't have to go back every morning," Elian said, and I grinned.

"Are you asking me to move in with you, Elian?"

"Of course. You're my mate, so we should live together, right?" he said, completely oblivious to the fact that most people considered moving in together to be a 'big step.'

"Yeah, you're right. I'll bring over some of my stuff tomorrow," I promised.

"Make sure to bring your collection of mementos and trinkets. I'll make space for them in the garden."

I smiled at his thoughtfulness and gave his hand another squeeze. I'd lucked out big time by getting a mate as sweet and amazing as Elian. All the years of loneliness had been so worth it if this was who I got to spend the rest of my life with.

When we got to the park, the first thing Elian did was remove his shoes. He truly hated them, didn't he? Then, he led us right to his garden. Apparently, he was done for the day. I was ready to sleep too, but there was one thing I wanted to do before we went to bed.

"Did you have fun tonight?" I asked as we stood in the middle of the garden, and Elian nodded.

"I did, yes. The food was amazing, and so was the restaurant. You made it so easy to be outside. Next time, I'd like to try going somewhere with people. Maybe some place that isn't too crowded?"

"Sure. We'll find something. We know quite a few people whom we can ask for suggestions too," I said, and Elian smiled.

"Can we sleep in our true forms tonight?" he asked after a moment, and I smiled.

"Sure, why not? But before that, there's something I wanted to give you."

"Give me? You mean like a present? You don't have to give me anything, Alden," he said, and I smiled as I stepped closer to him.

"This is for me as much as it's for you, okay?" I said, and Elian's brows furrowed as he slowly nodded.

Smiling, I removed the leather cord that hung around my neck, and Elian's eyes widened as they slid from me to the piece of my horn hanging between us.

"I would like you to wear this," I said, and Elian shook his head.

"I can't wear that! That's yours. How will you use your powers without it?"

"I can still use some of them," I assured him. "And I don't use them all that often anyway. I can shift without it too."

"But...why do you want me to wear it?"

"Humans get married and wear rings to show their commitment to each other. Since we're mates, we don't need to get married, but I'd like to give you this part of myself as a sign of my commitment," I explained, and the furrow between his brows cleared.

"Oh. If that's the case, I'd be honored to wear it," he said, and I smiled as I slid the cord around his neck.

Elian reached up and brushed his fingers against the horn while his eyes stayed on me, and a gasp slipped past his lips.

"What does red mean?" he asked, and I smiled.

"Love."

Closing what little distance there was between us, I pressed my lips to his as his hand dropped to his side. I'd thought long and hard about giving the piece of my horn to Elian, but I couldn't think of anywhere else it would be better protected. I wanted Elian to have it because he already had the rest of me.

Elian

I couldn't believe Alden had given such an important part of himself to me. I was going to make sure no harm ever came to it. I also wanted to give Alden something, but what?

An idea struck, and as we pulled away, I dropped the hands that'd somehow ended up holding onto Alden's waist and took a step back.

Alden gave me a curious look, and I smiled before shifting into my true form.

"Stop," I said when Alden started shifting too, and he reverted back to his human form. "Wait a minute, please."

I held my hand out, and Alden placed his in mine without hesitation. Holding my other hand up, I grew three roots out of my fingers and braided them around his wrist, infusing the fibre and wood with my magic so it wouldn't dry or break off. Once the bracelet was done, I disconnected the roots from me, leaving them to finish weaving around each other with the remainder of my power so there wouldn't be any loose ends.

"Wow. It...it feels like you, like your aura," Alden murmured, and I glanced at him.

"You can still see auras?"

"Only very faintly. But I'd recognize yours even if I was blind," Alden said, sending happy sparks shooting through my body.

"Would you like to sleep now?" I asked, and Alden smiled.

"In a minute."

Taking a step forward, he placed his hand on my cheek and kissed me, stunning me to my core. We'd never kissed like this, with me in my true form and Alden in his human form. It felt strange, but no less wonderful.

I kissed Alden back, and his lips curved against mine. I wrapped my arms around him, pulling him close, and he went willing. In this form, our heights were almost the same, and I could easily continue kissing him even with our chests pressed together.

When we finally pulled away, I realized the roots on my arms had somehow woven together. Probably because I'd been thinking about holding Alden close and never wanting to let go.

"Oops," I said as Alden noticed that he'd been basically tied up. "Give me a moment."

"You can tie me up anytime, Elian," Alden said with a wink, and I rolled my eyes.

Untangling the roots clinging to him, I stepped back, and Alden smiled before leaning forward once again.

"What are you—" Alden cut me off with a kiss, then rested his forehead against mine.

"I love you, Elian. I don't think I've said that enough times. I love you, I love you, I love you."

I laughed as he repeated the words over and over again, and then it was my turn to cut him off with a well-placed kiss.

"And I love you, my pirate, my very sweet unicorn. But I'm also very tired, so can you please shift so we can sleep?" I asked, and he stepped back before giving me a shallow bow.

"As you wish, my lord," he teased before quickly shifting into his true form.

We curled up on my makeshift mattress, and I hummed softly as Alden's heat filled me to the core. I didn't feel cold in this form, but his warmth still felt nice.

"Good night, Alden," I murmured, and he huffed softly in reply. Smiling to myself, I let sleep drag me away, knowing that

the best of my dreams couldn't get much better than the life I
was already looking forward to.

EPILOGUE

One Year Later

Elian

A year after meeting Alden, after discovering what true happiness felt like, I was ready to face the biggest hurdle of my life: a Mistvale clan lunch party.

It had taken me twelve whole months to feel brave enough to try, and I was one step away from chickening out once again.

I'd met practically every member of the clan sometime or the other, but the thought of hanging out with them all at once still seemed pretty damned overwhelming. I was going to do it, though, because I didn't want to get stuck in a metaphorical park again.

By now, Alden and I split our time pretty evenly between the park and our house. Not the one he'd shared with Memphis and his family, though.

Six months ago, Alden had purchased a cute little house in what he called a 'cul-de-sac.' Quill and his mates lived close by too, and while they were part of the reason Alden had bought the place, the other reason was that the house backed up to the park. I'd managed to convince the land in our home's backyard to accept me, so now we could be in our home without leaving my park, though we still enjoyed sleeping in the garden in our true forms.

"Hey, you okay?" Alden asked, and I nodded before I'd fully processed his question. "Are you freaking out? We can skip if you want, you know that, right?"

"I know. I want to go," I said definitively, and Alden smiled.

"All right. Well then, before that, I need to show you something," he said, and taking my hand, he led me back inside the house.

"What is it?" I asked when we stepped into the kitchen, and Alden pointed me toward a chair.

I sat down and waited patiently as he picked up a sheaf of papers from the counter and placed it in front of me. It looked like a deed of some kind, but all the legal language went right over my head.

"What is this?" I asked, confused.

"This," Alden said, sitting in the chair beside me and turning it so he was facing me, "is the deed to your park. It's in your name."

I blinked, unable to process what he'd said. I...owned my land? Legally? But how was that possible?

"I don't have any kind of documents. Or money. How did you...?"

"Raiden has a contact who makes fake documents. And I have money, Elian. More than I'll ever be able to spend in this lifetime," Alden said, his voice kind and so so full of love.

"You bought the park for me?" I repeated, and Alden shook his head.

"I made sure no one will be able to try to steal your land from you again. I'm sorry it took so long, but since we were buying from the government, I figured it wouldn't hurt to make sure all the documents were as clean as they could be," Alden said, and while I had no idea what that meant, I understood that Alden had spent the past year working on this. For me.

Carefully placing the papers back on the table, I slid forward in my chair and threw my arms around Alden. He caught me when I slipped off the chair in my haste, and placed me on his lap, my legs thrown on either side of his. Burying my face in his neck, I breathed in his warm, fresh scent as I tried to control the feelings rushing through me.

I'd loved Alden with my whole heart for a while now, but right then, it didn't feel like it was enough. I wished there was some way I could tell Alden exactly how much this meant to me.

Remembering that maybe there was, I sat back and took his hand in mine. He watched me curiously as I brought it up and wrapped it around the piece of his horn still hanging around my neck.

Realizing what I was trying to do, he gripped the horn on his own, and then gasped softly. "Oh, Elian."

"Thank you," I murmured, wishing the words were enough but knowing they were nowhere close. After what Alden had done for me, there was no way I wasn't going to that party.

"It was my pleasure, Elian. And it was also a little selfish," Alden said, and I had to give him a look of disbelief at that. How could this be selfish in any way? "See, if you're happy, I'm happy. And if something were to put your land at risk, you wouldn't be happy. So technically, I did this for my own happiness."

"Of course. How silly of me to think you did it for me," I said with a shake of my head, making him grin.

"Very silly," he agreed, and I smacked his chest. "Ow! Hey, now. Where did all that love go?"

"It's right here, my pirate. But loving someone means making sure they know when they're being an ass," I informed him, and he chuckled.

"Is that so? Well then, thank you for loving me so well," he said, and while he'd started with the same teasing grin, by the time he spoke the last word, his expression had softened into something much more gentle.

"I do love you," I said, then got to my feet and held my hand out to him. "Now let's go attend that party."

Alden

Elian was doing great. I knew he'd been worried about not being able to handle it, but he hadn't needed to. The others also seemed to be trying their best not to overwhelm him, and so far, all the party-related shenanigans had been kept to a minimum.

"But it's so unfair!" Cam whined as he dragged Micah behind him, and I wondered if it was the same complaint he'd had since those two discovered they had more mates. "Why do we have to wait until we're eighteen? Why do we get to pick and choose which human rules to follow?"

"Uh, because this one makes sense? If we found the other two and they're adults, we still couldn't be with them until we were eighteen. So what's the point?" Micah replied in a tone that implied he wasn't saying it for the first time.

Elian raised a brow at me, clearly having heard every word too, and I shook my head. There was no point in intervening because Cam knew very well that his dads wouldn't budge on that point, and also that they shouldn't. He just liked to complain sometimes.

"Hey, Elian," Jai said as he walked over with a plate of food in his hand, and Raphael close behind.

"Jai, Raphael, it's nice to see you again," Elian greeted them, and I smiled when they glanced my way. Today, I was planning to hang back and let Elian hold the floor, let him have the full experience. Unless he asked me to step in, of course.

"So, say, Elian...when someone visits your park and you aren't physically there, can you still see them?" Raphael asked, and something in his voice made me turn my focus back to them.

"I can if I want to, or if I'm passing through the trees around them," Elian said, and Raph made a "huh" sound. "I know you've visited the park quite a few times, if that's what you're asking."

"Kind of," Jai hedged, and my curiosity grew. What were these two digging at?

"Are you wondering about the times when you came to the park just the two of you, a few years ago?" Elian asked, and my eyes ping-ponged between the equally guilty looks on Jai and Raph's faces.

"What the hell did you two do at Elian's park?" I demanded, curious and unsure if I should be offended on Elian's behalf.

"In our defense, we didn't exactly know it was Elian's back then," Jai said.

"And we were a horny, newly mated couple," Raphael added.

"Angel!" Jai exclaimed, his tan skin going a few shades darker, and Elian broke into laughter. He'd known what they were trying to get at the whole time, hadn't he?

"I actually didn't see anything. The tree was traumatized, though," Elian said with a look of utter innocence on his face, and Jai's eyes went wide with horror.

"We're very sorry," he said, then smacked Raph's arm when he didn't say anything.

"Yeah, yeah. Very sorry," Raphael concurred, and Elian smiled.

"It's okay. The tree's probably already forgotten all about it," he assured them.

Once they'd drifted off to talk to someone else, I pulled Elian into my arms. "You're a sneaky one, Pan. These people have no idea about the wicked side you hide behind that innocent face."

"Are you going to tell them?" he asked, and I chuckled.

"Hell no. I love it."

"And I love you," Elian said, making me smile.

"I love you too. Every part of you."

The Mistvale adventure will continue in the next Mistvale series, Heirs of Mistvale, in 2024. Pre-order book one, Cam, Micah, and their mates' story, or sign up to Stella's newsletter to get a sneak peek at the first chapter!

AUTHOR'S NOTE

Dear reader,

Thank you so much for giving my Mistvale town a chance. I hope you've enjoyed all the stories set in this beautiful rainy town.

Don't worry, I'm not done with Mistvale yet, but I'll be taking a small break from Mistvale. I'm hoping to release Cam, Micah, and their mates' story in the third quarter of 2024. I will be releasing a short story set in Mistvale in February, though, so keep an eye out for that!

As a reader, you know as well as I do that every rating and review matters. Reviews mean the world to indie authors like me, so if you enjoyed reading this story—or even if you thought it could've been better—I'd love it if you could drop a short review on Amazon and/or Goodreads. It'd mean the world to me, and help me continue to write more books!

Love,
Stella.

JOIN ME ON PATREON!

Join me on Patreon and get exclusive access to:

- Access to my **first drafts**. (four new chapters every week!)

- Read an exclusive serial, ***The Prince's Mate***. (three chapters every month!)

- Access to audiobooks before everyone else. Listen to **all my audiobooks** for just $12!

- Ability to **make important decisions** about my upcoming books

- Special bonus scenes and **peeks into the lives of old characters**

- Early blurb and cover reveal

- Ability to **create your own character** that I'll write into a book

- **Exclusive merch**: stickers, prints, mugs, and more!

Join Stella on Patreon at patreon.com/authorstellarainbow

HAVE YOU READ ALL THE MISTVALE STORIES YET?

Read about Jai, Raphael, Cassian, Gustave, Aeron, and Niall in the **Mages of Mistvale** series:

Read about Devon, Oliver, Firey, Jules, Joy, Quill, and Tate in the **Misfits of Mistvale** series:

Read about Noel, Caleb, William, Raiden, Westley, Birch, Celeste, and Hector in **The Mistvale Spin-off Collection**:

Or revisit them all in a massive Christmas celebration in **Christmas in Mistvale:**

STELLA RAINBOW

ALSO BY STELLA

PARANORMAL ROMANCE

Set in Mistvale

Mages of Mistvale:
Set in the fictional town of Mistvale, Mages of Mistvale (previously Mages of Ravenshire) is a series filled with magic, laughs and love. Low on angst and high on sweetness, Mages of Mistvale will leave you with a smile on your face. Come meet Neya, Pads, April, and all the other fur-babies and their humans, vampires and mages. *If you're new to the town of Mistvale, this is where you start!*

Touch of Magic. (Raphael x Jai)

Sleep of Eternity. (Cassian x Gus)

Angel of Death. (Aeron x Niall)

Boxset.

Misfits of Mistvale:
With side-characters from Mages of Ravenshire, this series
features shifters, half-mermen, werewolves, and many more
supernaturals. With the usual dose of fur-babies, found family,
and all the Mistvale feels, this series features standalones with
a different couple in each book.

Claws. (Devon x Oliver)

Tails. (Jules x Firey)

Bonds. (Joy x Quill x Tate)

Boxset.

Mistvale Spin-Off Novellas:
Featuring various side-characters from the town of Mistvale,
these novellas are full of sweet, fluffy romance, and the med-
dlesome cast of Mistvale.

My Elf Mate. (Noel x Caleb)

My Dragon Mate. (Raiden x William)

My Elf Daddy. (Daddy/little, Westley x Birch)

My Fae Mate. (Genderfluid MC, Celeste x Hector)

Make A Wish. (Free read, Kezan x Ezra)

Christmas In Mistvale. (Revisit ALL your favorite Mistvale couples and see how they're doing!)

The Mistvale Spin-off Collection (Includes My Elf Mate, My Dragon Mate, My Elf Daddy, and My Fae Mate.)

Mystics of Mistvale:
Featuring some new residents of Mistvale, this series includes a single dad incubus, an elusive griffin, a wise unicorn, a protective gargoyle, and some more unique supes. And of course, you'll revisit some of your beloved Mistvalers from the previous books. With the usual dose of romance, found family, and all the Mistvale feels, this series features standalones with a different couple in each book.

The Elusive Griffin. (Memphis x Orion)

The Vulnerable Human. (Vo x Trick)

The Reclusive Dryad. (Alden x Elian)

Set in Otherworld

Fate's Gambit Trilogy:
Fate's Gambit is an MMM PNR trilogy featuring a sweet, subby cinnamon-bun devil, a gentle-giant who's a service sub/Daddy switch, and a slightly frustrated Master as they slowly figure our their dynamic and fall madly in love. They're joined by annoyingly awesome side-characters including a sweet hedgehog, a sassy talking snake, and a guardian in the form of a cat-man. This trilogy features the same triad: **Damien, Reece, & Artemus**, and needs to be read in order.

First Play. (Free Prequel.)

Devil's Gamble.

Pet's Ploy.

Master's Design.

Boxset.

Lords of Otherworld:

Following the events of Fate's Gambit, Lords of Otherworld delves deeper into the workings of Otherworld, with new characters, new romance, and new adventures. With found family vibes, danger and romance, each book in this series follows a different couple, with an overarching storyline. It is recommended to read the books in order.

Maximus

Zane.

Nox.

Lionel.

Standalones:

Healing Holiday.

Set in The Human Realm

Innocent Monsters:

Set in the human realm, this series is a spin-off from the Lords of Otherworld series, featuring the monsters you met in Nox. Find out how the wendigo, kraken, wyvern, troll, and kelpie find their HEA in this series. All books are standalones and can be read in any order.

Salvation.

Liberation.

Conviction.

Redemption.

Demon Debacles:
Demons have never lived in the human realm without their summoner. *Until now.*
Free to be themselves for the first time in centuries, these demons need magic—and some help from Fate—to figure out how to live their new lives to the fullest.

My Demon Roommates(MMMM)

The Sanctuary: Forest:
Home to a variety of supes who can't live—or don't want to—in the human world, The Sanctuary is a pocket realm run by sorcerer Zephyr Morrigan. This series features the residents of the Forest area within The Sanctuary.

The Naga

Standalones

Summoning Chaos (A demon x human novella.)

He Set Me Free (A newsletter serial.)

CONTEMPORARY ROMANCE

Voice Out

Weathering The Storm (Roommates to lovers, hurt/comfort.)

Watching The Sunrise (Friends to lovers, genderfluid MC.)

Weaving The Stars (Roommates to lovers, age gap, drag performer MC.)

AUDIOBOOKS

(Available in multiple audiobook stores! Buy straight from Stella's website for just $5.99!)

Lords of Otherworld

Maximus

Zane.

Nox.

Lionel.

ABOUT STELLA

Stella Rainbow lives in a small town in India with her family and her five-year-old cat, Harry, who is her number one supporter, cuddle buddy, and writing buddy all rolled into one. Living with a chronic illness, Stella grew up with books as her best friends, and now she writes in the hopes of giving others like her a reprieve from the real world.

Stella's books are low on the angst, high on the sweetness, with a doze of found family, and some absolutely adorable fur—and sometimes scale—babies.

You can join her mailing list to receive updates about her books and free content. You can also read more about Stella, her books, and the universe she writes in on her website, www.authorstellarainbow.com.

If you'd like to hang out with her, you can also join her Facebook group, **Stella's Mistvalers**.

Subscribe to her **Patreon** to get access to her books as she writes them, get audiobooks at heavily discounted prices, exclusive stories, and much more!

You can also follow her on:
Facebook: Stella Rainbow
Goodreads: Stella Rainbow
BookBub: Stella Rainbow

Amazon: <u>Stella Rainbow</u>